HIDING IN MONTANA

CLEAN WESTERN ROMANCE SUSPENSE

COWBOYS OF RIVER JUNCTION
BOOK TWO

LUCINDA RACE

COPYRIGHT

Editor Kimberly Dawn
Cover design by Jody Kaye

Manufactured in the United States of America
First Edition January 2023
Print Edition 978-1-954520-42-4
E-book ISBN 978-1-954520-47-1

AUTHOR NOTE

Hi and welcome to my world of romance. I hope you love my characters as much I do. So, turn the page and fall in love again.

If you'd like to stay in touch, please join my Newsletter. I release it twice per month with tidbits, recipes and an occasional special gift just for my readers so sign up here: https://lucindarace.com/newsletter/ and there's a free book when you join!

Happy reading...

---

*Q*UICK NOTE: If you enjoy Hiding in Montana, be sure to check out my offer for a FREE Price Family novella at the end. With that, happy reading!

***

Polly Carson stuck her leather work gloves in the back of her faded Levis. She sat back on her heels, surveying the row of tomato plants she had just mulched. Rubbing the ache in her lower back reminded her she wasn't twenty anymore. Looking at her surroundings, she wouldn't change life on Grace Star Ranch for anything in the world. Working the land in Montana had been a dream come true, and it put her in close proximity to Clint Goodman, the only man who made her heart skitter in her chest with just a smile. Not that he even recognized her. No one could. But she knew he had a good heart. What person would happen along, find a woman so badly broken that he'd stay with her, and even visit her in the hospital? She remembered little about those first days, but she remembered his voice, the deep dimples, and sable-brown eyes, and the way he talked about his home, Grace Star Ranch, had sounded like heaven on earth.

She touched her face, picturing her reflection in the mirror. The plastic surgeon had done an amazing job of putting her back together. The only scars that remained were on the inside. She shook off the darkness that threatened to obscure the July sunshine and stood up. This morning she woke in a cold sweat, her heart racing from the same nightmare she'd had for the last three years. She was running and her feet gave way, sliding down a rocky embankment. Helpless. Ending in a heap at the bottom of a ravine. But it hadn't been a dream. It had been what brought her to this point, even though she remembered nothing after she had breakfast until they found her. Until Clint found her. Even now, her heart pounded in her chest as it tightened with the familiar panic. Taking several deep cleansing breaths, she reminded herself nothing would get done dwelling on the past. She knew better than anyone life could change in an instant.

The sound of someone calling her name interrupted her thoughts. Annie, the owner of the ranch and her boss, was headed in her direction.

"Morning," she called out. "How's things going out here?" She popped her hands on her hips and took in the massive garden. "It's amazing what you've done in just a year." She bent over and tore off a lettuce leaf, inspecting it, and then popping it in her mouth. "Nothing like from garden to mouth."

Polly liked Annie. Her openness and willingness to listen and implement new ideas was just one reason working here was the best job she'd ever had. "The critters would devour the lettuce if we hadn't installed that fencing."

"I'm glad Clint and the boys could get it done before everything grew."

Polly turned away so Annie couldn't see her cheeks get pink at the mere mention of his name. "Chicken wire did the trick, that's for sure."

"Tell me, what's the scoop with these tomato plants? They're already a foot tall and deep green, nothing like what I saw down at The Trading Post a few days ago."

"I grew these in the greenhouse. We've got a grape variety and ones that will ripen in our short growing season. Quinn's already thinking about how many quarts he can process for the winter."

Annie shuddered. "We just got over that season. I'm not ready to start thinkin' about snow." Her soft twang only came out occasionally, but Polly liked it.

With a soft laugh, she said, "It's part of growing food. We need to think about the harvest and preserving it. Besides, we have a pleasant summer coming up since our spring has been warm. It's a good indicator we're in for a stretch of sunny days ahead."

"Do you think you'll have enough greenhouse space to grow even more for next year? With the resort having a soft opening in the fall, I'm hopeful we will book the cabins solid next summer."

Annie had part of the ranch under construction with six family-style cabins and an expansion to the horse stable. Her plan was to add a dude ranch resort as an offshoot of the cattle business. Daphne, her friend from Boston, had moved out to run it.

"Not to worry, I'm using this year's harvest as a gauge of what we'll need to expand for next year. Feeding the ranch hands and preserving what we can is a part of the overall plan. You'll need to decide how meals will run for the resort, are guests eating with the hands, or is there a separate dining hall? If Jed's going to oversee everything, then he has ideas about the menu. I guess what I'm saying is, it's an open-ended discussion until we know if Quinn is the head chef or if you are having two separate kitchens."

Annie tapped her chin with her index finger and turned her head in the direction of the dining hall. "I've been putting off this conversation long enough. I'll run down and talk to Quinn this morning. I was hoping he'd come to me and ask for the head chef job, but maybe he's waiting for me to offer it." With a shake of her head, she grinned. "He's strong and silent like a few of our men around here."

Polly instantly thought of Clint. He was the strong, silent type, steady as her heartbeat, well, until he occupied space with her, and then her heart thumped wildly. She really needed to stop crushing on that man.

"And you have a few raucous ones down there, too. Clint had Zak Dawson up helping with the fence and all he did was crack jokes."

Her eyes grew wide. "Clint or Zak?"

Her cheeks grew warm. "Zak's the funny man of that duo." But Clint had the occasional one-liner that cracked her up, too. Not that she was about to tell Annie that.

"Zak's a good man and even better with the horses. He probably tires of not having people to talk with, so he makes up for it." Annie gave her a sharp look. "Clint's got a good sense of humor. He just keeps it on the down low until he really gets to know someone."

She dipped her head and looked at Annie. "Thanks, I'll keep that in mind."

4

"Hey, can you do me a favor before you head out?" Annie glanced back at the main house. "Mary's a little tired today. Would you cut some lettuce and if there are radishes, harvest some for dinner tonight and drop them at the house? I have to run into town and I'd feel better knowing someone had laid eyes on her while I'm gone."

"Is she alright?"

"If you ask her, yes, still running this place like my Pops were still alive. But she picked up a cold, and it's settled in her chest, and we both know Mary, stubborn as a mule about resting. She'll be down here when she gets ready to fix dinner, getting what she can and well…" Her voice trailed off.

Polly saw the tears well up and then get blinked away from Annie's eyes. "Consider it done. Maybe we can have tea together and I can pick her brain about her success with the garden all these years."

"I tried to tell her I'd"—she gave a sheepish grin and shrugged her shoulders—"well, Linc would cook tonight, but she insists on fixing supper."

"My grandma was just like Mary, never wanting help. At least Mary's relinquished most of the gardening to me. She even allowed me to work in her flower gardens."

Annie placed a warm hand on Polly's arm. "I really appreciate your patience with Mary. She's the only family I have left."

"We all love her, so stop worrying. I can pop in whenever for a quick glass of water." She patted the small walkie-talkie on her hip. "And you can reach me anytime."

Polly would do just about anything for Annie and her family. After all, if it wasn't for the woman standing in front of her, Polly wouldn't be living her dream or live in close proximity to the man who had saved her life. One of these days, she needed to fess up and tell him who she was and thank him.

"I got lucky when Jeremy introduced us at The Trading Post."

Polly swallowed the lump in her throat; she knew exactly what Annie meant. It was a fresh start for both of them—Annie taking over the family's ranch and her working at the ranch. They were both building a new life from the ground up.

"Hey, how often is a gardener given the chance to start an entire operation literally from just a patch of land and an idea?"

Annie shrugged. "Like every spring?"

"Nope, this land needed to be cultivated and coaxed back into life. We've added compost and fertilizer, turned in nutrients, and let the magic of nature work over the winter." Much like her transformation as she worked the land, it restored her faith that the future was bright. She had left the withered version of herself on that hiking trail.

"You did the work." Annie gave her a bright smile.

In more ways than just the plot of land in front of them. "Thanks, Annie. All I needed was the opportunity."

Her smile grew. "Oh, look, there's Clint and Linc."

The two cowboys headed in their direction. Clint was taller and thinner than his boss, who was also Annie's husband, but they both had dark hair and the muscles of a hard-working cowboy. That's where the similarities ended. Linc's smile was quick and easy, whereas Clint's was slow and guarded. He was slowly getting comfortable around her, but it had puzzled Polly why.

"Ladies," Linc said and pecked his wife's lips. "I thought I'd find you out here, Annie."

"Actually, I was talking with Polly about plans for next year, and then I'm on my way down to see Quinn."

Clint gave Polly a half grin. "Gotta feel sorry for the cook. Once Annie says she's gonna talk to someone, that means they'd best be prepared to make some decisions."

Although her tongue felt like she'd trip over it if she spoke, she laughed and then said, "I think I'd been in that same position last year."

He pushed his Stetson back on his head and gave her a rare, wide smile. "And look how that turned out. We're now eating better than ever, thanks to your skills."

She could feel the flush rise in her cheeks and she eked out, "That's nice of you to say."

"Wouldn't say it if I didn't mean it." Clint's deep drawl made her toes curl in her work boots.

Polly could feel Annie's eyes watching them as they bantered. She chanced a quick look, and Annie's eyes widened with laughter. But it left her questions unasked. Polly was sure that would be a topic of conversation when they talked later.

"Linc, why don't we head down to the dining hall? I think Polly was going to ask Clint for some help with something." Annie gave Polly a sly wink and slipped her arm through her husband's.

"Clint, after you're done up here, can you stop down at the horse barn and check on things there? I have some things to go over with Annie in the office."

Polly noticed the glint in Linc's eyes and if she were to hazard a guess, this was part of Annie and Linc's not-so-subtle way of playing matchmaker.

"You got it, and then I'm gonna check on the new

calves. Doc Howard will be making a quick trip out later too."

"Good." Linc took Annie's hand and with a smile in Polly's direction and a curt nod to Clint, he said, "Take all the time Polly needs to get whatever done."

When they were out of earshot, Clint stuck his hands in his front pockets and rocked back in his boots. He was studying Polly carefully. "So, how can I help you?"

2

*C*lint always had the vague feeling that he knew the woman standing in front of him. But he couldn't quite extract the memory. Polly was beautiful—a little taller than the average girl, slender, probably from hard work in the gardens, long reddish-brown hair, and those hazel eyes. They held a hint of a smile in them, which tripped his trigger, that's for sure. If only he could remember where he had seen her. It had plagued him for almost a year, so he was just gonna stop trying.

"Annie said you needed help with something?"

Polly chewed the corner of her lip and looked around the fenced-in garden. "Not at the moment. We were talking about the greenhouse. Maybe in a few weeks, you can see if one of the guys can help me build some new compost bins closer to the back entrance. Camouflage them from the future guests."

That's when Clint realized Annie put him and Polly on the hot seat. Why was it every time newly married people saw a couple of singles talking, they instantly thought of pairing them off? Like couples on Noah's Ark. Maybe it was the sizzle between them. Heck, if Polly didn't seem fazed by it, then maybe it wasn't a big deal after all, just a one-sided attraction.

"Well, you know where to find me, and if everyone's busy, I'm always ready to lend a hand if you need it." He lingered, waiting to see if there was anything else she might say, but she remained silent. The uncomfortable silence weighed down on them. "I'll take off now."

Polly looked away and then back at him. Her eyes locked on his. "I appreciate the offer, Clint."

The way she said his name was like a gut punch and an embrace at the same time, and it had been like this since the first day he'd helped her plow up the land and set the fencing.

"Anytime." He strode away, but he could feel her eyes on his back. He stopped, looked over his shoulder, and strode back to where she was still standing.

"Polly, any chance you want to meet me some night at The Lucky Bucket for supper?"

Her eyes grew wide, as if she'd never been asked out for a meal before. "What about Annie?"

Where did that come from? "Are you saying I should ask Annie for dinner?"

"No," she stammered, "She might have a policy against people sitting down and having supper together."

That sounded like the lamest rejection he'd ever heard. "Like a policy for people who work on the ranch can't date?"

She nodded, but she kept her wide hazel eyes locked on his. If he didn't know better, he'd swear he saw a hint of fear in them.

"Are you saying if you knew for sure, you might consider it?"

She shrugged. "Maybe?"

That was better than an outright no. "I'll talk to Linc and see what he says and I'll get back to you. So think about it. Just a couple of friendly co-workers sharing a bite. No strings." He threw that out there and saw a spark of something recede in her eyes. She couldn't be afraid of him, could she?

"Great, thanks, and well, um, I'll see ya around."

He walked off in the direction of the horse barn, determined to find out if there was a no dating policy among ranch workers. And if there was, he was going to see what he could do to change it. There was something about Polly that drew him in like a bee to wildflowers.

Clint saw Linc walking in his direction and he was going to find out if Annie had rules for him dating Polly.

"Clint, why the serious expression?" Linc looked around the horse barn. "Busy day?"

"A mite. I've been rustling something over in my head, and I have to ask, does Annie have any rules about co-workers dating?"

"Are you talking about someone specific who might work for the ranch, or is this hypothetical?" He pushed the brim of his hat back and his grin grew wide.

His old friend was going to make him shoot straight. "I asked Polly if she wanted to meet me at the Bucket for supper some night, and she said there might be something that Annie had in place so we couldn't." He scuffed his boot and kicked a small bundle of hay skittering across the cement floor.

"Well, if she had, that rule was shot to the devil with not only us dating, but we got married to boot." Linc clamped his hand on Clint's shoulder. "I'd say you're safe to take the woman out."

With a slow shake of his head, he said, "I'll ask Annie just to be sure."

"You really like this woman. I've never seen you get so riled up around a pretty face before."

Hooking his thumbs in his belt loops, Clint leaned back against the wall. "From the first moment I laid eyes on her, I felt like we'd met, but I've racked my brain and come up with nothing. But the pull is still there." This was unfamiliar territory for him. He dated but let no one get too serious, except for one time. He had a job he loved and he lived on the nicest ranch in Montana. He wasn't about to let a woman change all that, and most wanted the picket fence, house with the sunny-yellow door, and a man who didn't have to work weekends.

"I get it, Clint, and from this viewpoint, you got it bad for this woman."

He nodded and felt his face fall. "That's why I want to take her out, see what's going on between us. I think she feels it too." He wiped his hands down his legs. "Heck, maybe it's just wishful thinking, but I've gotta try, right?" Out of all his buddies, Linc would understand what he was trying to say. When all hope was lost with him and Annie, they put their stubborn pride aside, talked, and found their way back to each other. They gave him hope he could have it all.

"I'm the first one to say go for it. I spent too many years not being honest with Annie and it cost us years together, so don't follow my lead." He pointed to the main house. "I know for a fact Annie's in her office and her door is always open. Go talk to her and find out straight from the boss' mouth that you're free to date whoever you want, and that includes the pretty Polly Carson."

~

*C*lint rapped on the doorjamb to Annie's office. She looked up from the paper she was reading and put it down, a welcoming smile on her face.

"Clint, come on in."

He entered through the glass door from the back patio of the house. He didn't want to carry in any dirt. And also, he didn't want Mary to know since she'd been poking at him all winter to cowboy up and ask Polly out on a proper date instead of mooning around the ranch. Her words, not his.

He swept his hat off his head and held it in his hands. "Got a minute to talk?"

She gestured to the chair opposite her. "Have a seat and tell me what's on your mind."

His gut tightened as he sat down. "I hope I'm not interrupting anything, but I was talking to Linc, and he suggested I come up."

Her smile reassured him it was more than okay. "When I took over the ranch after Pops died, I said his longstanding open-door policy was going to remain the same with me and I meant it." She folded her hands together and leaned forward and just waited.

It surprised him she didn't have questions, but remained patient until he was ready to talk. But he wasn't sure how to begin.

"Clint, I'm a firm believer that when you're struggling to share what's on your mind, it's best to start at the beginning."

He swallowed hard. "You're right. I like Polly."

She smiled with a nod. "I might have noticed the looks between the two of you."

13

Did Annie just say that Polly was looking at him, too? "Well, today, after you and Linc left us, I asked her if she wanted to meet me at The Lucky Bucket sometime. She mentioned you might have a policy against co-workers spending time together."

To Annie's credit, she didn't grimace or laugh. "I appreciate you coming to talk with me, but I don't believe in restricting who my employees date. But I would ask if you two decide to start something and it doesn't work out to be professional when working together. But your personal life is just that, personal, to do as you wish."

He felt as if an enormous weight had slipped from his shoulders. They were free to go out and spend time together. "That's great. Thanks, Annie." He stood up, and she held out her hand as if stopping him. He sank back into the chair.

"I'm not one to pry into anyone's life. It's just not my way. Take it at Polly's pace. I get the feeling she's been through some tough patches in her past and I want what's best for you both."

He toyed with his hat in his hands and nodded. He understood what she meant. There was something fragile in her eyes and the last thing he'd do was rush Polly into anything. "You don't have to worry. I care a lot about her." As he spoke those words, he realized just how accurate they were. He wanted to get to know Polly and have fun, put a smile on her face, and just live in the moment.

"You're a good man and if Polly agrees to date you, well, you're both very lucky."

Now he stood up and grinned at his boss. She was a lot like her grandfather. "Pops would be proud of you, since I'm pretty sure he would have handled this conversation much the same way."

She pushed her chair back and stood up. "Thank you. I'm trying to make him proud of me, even as he's looking down on the ranch from heaven." She tipped her head. "I'm curious. What did Linc say to you about dating?"

He chuckled. "Pretty much what you said, and he tossed into the mix that the two of you not only dated, but got hitched to boot."

"I married a very smart man, but do me one favor and pick Polly up like a proper date. Don't ask her to meet you there. And Clint, my door is open to all employees, and this wasn't the first conversation I had on this topic today." She gave him a knowing wink. "The last time I saw Polly, she was headed in the direction of the greenhouse."

That was the only prod he needed. After saying goodbye to Annie, he strode out the door. He scanned the fenced-in garden and didn't see anyone. It was then he noticed her old truck puttering down the road that would go past the main house in less than two minutes, and if he hurried, he could still catch her.

He rounded the corner and held up his hand to flag Polly down. She stopped the truck and put it in park before the driver's window was cranked down.

"Hey, Clint. What's going on?"

He jerked his thumb toward the house. "I just talked to Annie and I'm about to ask you a question for the second time. Will you have dinner with me at The Lucky Bucket?"

3

_P_olly knew Clint would seek her out as soon as he discovered dating was back on the table. It was all she had thought about over the last few hours. The silence seemed to weigh heavy between them and she knew there was only one answer she wanted to give. She just hoped she wouldn't regret it. "I'd like that."

His face lit up like the midday sun. "That's great. When? Thursday night?"

Her thoughts raced. That would give her two days to come up with the perfect outfit for a casual dinner with a drop-dead gorgeous man. "Sounds good. What time should I meet you there?"

"If you don't mind, I'd like to pick you up. My momma would have a fit if she knew I was taking a beautiful woman out for dinner and she drove herself."

Did he just call her beautiful or was it a slip of the tongue? "Sure, I live out on Dry Creek Road. At the south end of Main Street, you take a left."

"I know the area; how's six?"

"That'd be nice. My house is the log cabin with deep-green shutters. It's the only log cabin, so I'll be easy to find." Her heart skipped, but she plowed ahead. She had gone this far; she might as well get his number too.

"Why don't you text me your cell number and that way we can reach out if something comes up?" Not that there was anything that would stop her from going out to dinner with Clint. This was something she had wanted but thought would never happen.

He withdrew his cell and handed it to her. "Why don't you put your number in and call yourself?"

"Efficient. I like it." She flashed him a grin and tapped her digits into a new contact and then dialed her cell so caller ID would register his number too. Once that was accomplished, she handed him his phone. "Alright, well, I'm gonna head home. It's been a busy day."

He took a step back from her truck and tapped the open window. "Drive carefully."

His heart-melting smile made her insides tingle. She fluttered her fingertips in a wave before she put the truck back into drive and pulled away from him. Looking in her rearview mirror, she could see him watching her leave, and he lifted his hand in one last wave before she went around the bend in the long driveway.

Once Clint was out of sight, she exhaled and then squealed with delight. She had a date and she couldn't wait. She glanced at the clock. In fifty hours, he'd be picking her up. The first thing she had to do when she got home was check her closet for the perfect outfit.

*P*olly looked in the mirror again. After trying on four different outfits, she settled on a Boho turquoise floral dress and brown cowboy boots. She added a heart-shaped turquoise necklace and large hoop earrings. The question she had was whether to leave her hair down or pull it back in a clip. Then she thought of the faint scars on her neck from a tube inserted after her accident and left it down. Better camouflage. Tonight was not the night to reveal her accident, which would only lead to more questions. That could cause this budding friendship to wither and die before it even had time to take root.

A sharp rap on her door snapped her out of the oppressive secret. She put a smile on her face and called out, "Coming!"

Clint was standing on her wide porch dressed in snug dark blue jeans, a crisp butter-colored shirt, and he held his hat in his hand. His gaze roamed from her eyes to her toes and he smiled appreciatively. "Evening, Polly. You look beautiful."

By the sparkle in his eyes, he thought she looked pretty good. "Other than the wedding, this is probably the only time you've seen me in a dress."

"It looks real nice, too."

"I'll just get my bag and we can leave."

He held out a brown paper sack. "I brought this for you. I know flowers are traditional for a date, but since you take care of the gardens, I thought you might have some here." He glanced at her yard. "I was right. I hope you like ice cream."

She opened the top of the bag and saw, in fact, there was ice cream and more. With a soft laugh, she asked, "What all is in here?"

"Fixings for banana splits, complete with nuts and whipped cream."

He beamed. She couldn't help it, so she took a step toward him and barely brushed her lips against his cheek. "Thank you. This was very thoughtful and completely unexpected." She bopped her head in the kitchen's direction. "Let me put this away and we can go."

Clint stood on the porch and never crossed the threshold while she hurried into the other room. In record time, she put everything in the freezer and refrigerator. When she came back out, he was still standing on the porch.

"Why didn't you come in?"

He looked her directly in the eye. "You didn't invite me."

Clint stated the reason so simply she was taken aback. "I'm sorry; that was rude of me."

He gave her that smile again and said, "Don't worry. When you do invite me in, you won't have to ask me twice."

That made her heart race with all that his statement could imply. But she was sure by the smile that filled his face and warmed his eyes she would be perfectly safe.

The door opened and Clint waited until she stepped onto the porch before he pulled the heavy wooden door closed tight. She put the key in the lock and made sure it was secured.

"I'm ready if you are?"

With his hand placed lightly in the curve of the small of her back, they walked to his truck and once again he held the door and offered his hand to help her inside. She never realized he was such a gentleman, a far cry from her ex who said unless she had a broken limb, he was never holding a door for her. His logic. No one had ever held a door for him.

Her smile dipped and Clint said, "Is everything okay? I only have one vehicle."

Now she felt like a jerk. This was their night, not for her to relive another unpleasant memory. "No, the truck is fine. I was just remembering something I had forgotten about."

Doubt remained on his face.

"Really, Clint. I will never lie to you, so when I tell you something, you can trust it."

He closed the passenger door and jogged around to the driver's side. "I'm hoping the Bucket won't be too busy tonight."

She appreciated his attempt to lighten the mood. The last thing she wanted was her past to intrude again. The ghosts were supposed to be vanquished. She had certainly spent enough time with the psychologist when she was in rehab after her discharge from the hospital.

With a laugh, she said, "All ready to get the night over with?"

"Oh, gosh, no. Not at all. I just didn't want you to have to wait."

He turned quickly to look at her and hopefully he'd realize she was trying to joke. "Clint, if they're busy, maybe we can sit outside? Annie mentioned they had a few tables along the front."

His face visibly relaxed and now he grinned, and those dimples appeared. "We can do whatever you'd like."

"How about we just play it by ear and let's see where the night takes us?" Her stomach flipped when she said that, when all she meant was where they would sit. But then her thoughts returned to the fixings for sundaes and there was the idea of asking him to stay for dessert.

"I thought you were a planner." He turned on Main Street and puttered down, scanning for parking spots.

Most of the spots were taken, which was odd since it was a Thursday. "I wonder what's going on downtown with so many people out tonight."

Clint slipped the truck into a vacant spot near the bar and grill and turned off the key. "We can wander down Main Street and check it out before dinner, if you'd like?"

"I love that idea." She hopped out of the truck before Clint even got his door opened. She really didn't want him to come around and open her door again and, if she was to guess, that was on his radar.

She waited for him at the back of the truck, and his expression was a tad serious.

"Polly, I know you're an independent woman, strong and more than capable. But I would really like it, when we're on a date, if I could hold the doors for you. It may sound old-fashioned, but it's something that's kind of important to me."

This was a wrinkle she hadn't expected, but she appreciated his forthright approach.

"I've never dated anyone with such impeccable manners. It's very sweet of you."

He held out the crook of his arm for her to place her hand in and wiggled his eyebrows. "Momma said if I learned nothing else from her, I needed to remember how to treat people with respect and kindness."

Polly tucked her hand in the crook of his arm and gave it a quick squeeze. "Who am I to argue with your mother?"

The couple walked the length of Main Street and

discovered there was a family concert in the town square. Children and adults alike were singing along with the troubadour and his band. They lingered in the back of the group for a couple of songs before turning back toward the bar.

"Hungry yet?" he asked her.

"One thing you'll learn about me is I'm always hungry." She laughed and felt lighter than she had in a long time. Not only was she having fun, but with Clint next to her, she didn't fear someone was lurking in the shadows. Not that her ex would ever expect to find her in a small town in Montana. It was light years away from Portland.

When they arrived at The Lucky Bucket Bar and Grill, Polly reached for the door handle and stopped, giving Clint a half smile. "This is going to take a little getting used to."

"I tell you what, I won't hold your chair for you."

Her mouth gaped open. "You do that too?"

He gave a slight bow and grinned. "But of course, it's part of Momma's course for impeccable manners."

Inside, there were a few patrons, and Polly suggested they take a booth. That way, there were no chairs to be held and they could hear each other talk. First date conversation was always a little stilted, but Clint wasn't the typical first date. They had officially met over a year ago now. Working at the ranch, they ran into each other from time to time.

After placing their drink orders for margaritas and a plate of nachos—her suggestion, not his—Polly leaned back and looked around the room. "It seems like everyone is at the concert."

"We've got the place to ourselves."

The server returned with their drinks and nachos and left them with the promise she'd be back to check on them.

Polly took a sip of the frozen drink and enjoyed the mix of sweet and salt from the rim of the glass. "This was a great idea. Thanks for asking me out tonight."

Clint waited until she filled a small plate with chips and fixings before saying, "I've been wanting to ask you out since last year, but I wasn't sure if you were interested in me."

"So, what made you take the plunge?" Again, his direct approach was refreshing.

"If I never asked, you couldn't say yes."

The simple answer was so like what she expected of Clint. "I always thought you were just being polite around me. I never expected this." She gestured to the space between them.

"I have to confess; ever since you started working at Grace Star Ranch, I've had the feeling we met at some point, but I think you mentioned you're from the west coast and I've never been out of Montana."

She choked on the chip and took a gulp of her margarita.

---

4

*C*lint got up and pulled Polly's hands over her head in an attempt to clear her airway as she choked on a chip. He was ready to haul her out of the booth and do the Heimlich maneuver if necessary.

She waved her hands and croaked. "I'm fine, just down the wrong pipe."

He handed her a paper napkin so she could wipe the tears on her cheeks. "Are you sure?"

The server rushed over. "Is everything okay here?"

Clint's eyes never left Polly's pale face. "Glass of water, please?"

The server grabbed a pitcher from a nearby table and filled a red plastic cup before handing it to him.

"Polly, can you breathe?" His heart hammered in his chest. He wasn't the best in medical emergency situations. He had his moments, but this was scaring the hell out of him.

She nodded and took the cup of water to take a tiny sip. With a tentative smile, she said, "I'm fine." Her smile grew wider, and she pointed to his side of the table. "Sit. Really, I'm okay."

He hesitated and then sat, but his eyes never left her face as it regained a healthy pink color and not that shade of white it had turned.

She smiled at the server, who still hovered close by. "Thanks. I'm okay." With eyes lowered, she said, "I really hate it when I'm the center of attention."

"Don't pay any attention to them. People were just concerned for you."

She shifted on the bench seat. "Can we talk about something else? Tell me why you wanted to be a cowboy."

He eased back in the chair. "What kid doesn't want to be a cowboy or firefighter growing up? I was raised here, and ranches are a way of life." He didn't like to talk about himself, but he wanted to know more about Polly, so he needed to share, too.

"Did you grow up on a ranch?"

"No, my parents have a grocery store in Springdale and they moved closer a few years back. My brother and sister and their families live there too. When I wanted to strike out on my own, I discovered Grace Star Ranch was looking to hire hands. I came and talked to Pops, Annie's grandfather. He hired me on the spot and the rest is history."

Her lips formed a perfect bow, and he wondered what it would be like to kiss her, but he focused on her question. "Why did everyone call Mr. Grace, Pops?"

"From what I heard, he said Mr. Grace was his grandfather, and they named him after his dad and didn't want to be confused with him either, so after Annie's dad was born, he just went by Pops and he is legendary."

She scrunched up her face and sipped her water. "I'm not sure I understand."

"Think of John Wayne, not the actor but the real man who lived by a strong code of ethics. Pops was that man you'd want as a son or brother. He and Pippa, his wife, they had the kind of marriage storybooks are written about. He could look anyone in the eye and he never flinched at honesty."

"I would like to have known him." Her voice was soft and her eyes wide.

Clint tapped the tabletop. "Annie's this generation's version of Pops. She's a lot like him, a straight shooter, and doesn't tolerate bullcrap. And she's loyal to the end."

"Good to know."

"Tell me about Portland. Is that where you grew up and is that when you started gardening?" They were falling back into the easy conversation where they started before Polly choked.

"I grew up in the Midwest and moved to Portland after college. I was working in advertising, nothing to get excited about, but Portland was a nice place to live. It was there my gardening hobby really took off."

"So how did you end up in our neck of the woods?" He leaned forward, knowing that Polly came to town a couple of years ago with no family or friends in the area.

"I came out to go hiking and fell in love with the area." Her cheeks flushed a deep pink. "When it was time for a change, this seemed like the best place to start over."

"I didn't know you enjoyed hiking. We can go sometime if you want." Sweet, something they could do together.

"I haven't been on the trails in about three years. To be honest, I had an accident and lost my nerve to be out there again." She looked away and down, but not before he saw the fear that hovered in her pretty hazel eyes.

"I'm sorry about that, but it brought you to River Junction, so out of something bad came something good."

She nodded. "True. Do you hike?"

"When I have free time and I can get some buddies to hit the trail with me. We usually head a few hours west. There are some good hiking areas farther out there, but recently I've stuck pretty close to home, spending long weekends with my folks. They're not getting any younger, and I love playing with my nieces."

She tipped her head to one side, and it was easy to see that talking about kids touched a soft spot in her. "Just girls, no boys?"

"Not so far, to Dad's dismay. Don't get me wrong, he loves his granddaughters, but he's old school and would love to have a grandson to carry on the Goodman name."

"I could see why he'd want that. I think every dad wants the name carried on, at least certain generations do."

He saw the server looking at them. "Do you want to order dinner or just have the nachos?"

"I could go for a burger and if you ask nice, I might share my fries with you." She gave him a sassy wink, and he liked how it caused a zing to race through him.

"How about we order fries and onion rings and we can share them?"

She grinned. "Sounds like an excellent compromise."

He signaled for the server. She came over and they placed their orders for burgers and sides.

Over an hour later, they were lingering over what was left of their dinner and Polly was sipping an iced tea. "That was delicious, but I should have saved half the burger for lunch tomorrow. I'm stuffed." Polly wiped her mouth on the paper napkin, but she missed a spot of ketchup on her cheek.

Clint pointed to it, and she wiped it off. He wanted to lean over and do it for her, but that would have been too forward and such a cliché. *Slow down, cowboy. This girl is a touch skittish, and you need to show her you're trustworthy.*

"If you're all done, we could go for another walk down the street or take a drive. I can show you some additional high points of our small town, or I can take you home."

She looked at him through her lowered lashes. "We should head back to my place. It's been a busy day and tomorrow it's going to be just as hectic at the ranch."

He kept his voice even to hide the disappointment that their date was ending. "Sure, another time."

She placed a hand over his, stopping him before he could signal for the check. "I've had a great time tonight. I hope we can do this again." Her shy smile was almost his undoing. He'd wanted to date her for such a long time that he'd take her anywhere she wanted to go. Just to spend time together was amazing.

Clint said, "I'd like that. Just tell me when you're free and we can go out again."

"I'll keep that in mind." She licked her lips. He guessed it was because of nerves and not an invitation for a kiss. He settled up the check and left a generous tip. On their way out the exit door, the server stopped them to double-check Polly wasn't suffering ill effects after choking earlier. But Polly reassured the girl she was fine and thanked the server for her quick response.

Polly held out her hand, and he took it while they strolled hand in hand for the short walk to the truck. Too bad it wasn't longer and much to his pleasant surprise, she waited until he opened the door and helped her in. He appreciated that she seemed to understand it was something important to him, and he hoped it showed she was special to him.

They rode in silence as the drive to her place went by way too quick. He was already wondering what they could do on their next date. He stopped in front of her house and turned the truck off. Would she want him to kiss her good night, or maybe she didn't kiss on the first date. He'd wait for a sign from Polly before making any kind of move. He didn't want to spook her like a new filly.

"I was thinking, if you're interested, we could have ice cream on the front porch. I just happen to have all the fixings right in my refrigerator."

Sitting on the porch was a perfect way to end the night. He could hear the light teasing tone in her voice and there was no way he'd say no to her invitation.

"That'd be a mighty nice way to end the evening." He opened the door and kept a steady speed as he walked around to open the door for her. He held out his hand to help her down, and she fell against his chest as the heel of her boot got caught on the running board.

"Don't worry, I won't let you fall."

Her eyelashes fluttered, and he heard her breath catch. She whispered, "Thank you."

They stood in the Montana moonlight with his arms wrapped around her. Polly didn't seem to be in a hurry to step out of them. The soft moonbeams seemed to shine just for them.

He cleared his throat. "Are you okay?"

Bobbing her head, she said, "Yes, I'm fine." Her laugh came out as a nervous giggle. "It seems I've said that a lot tonight." She eased back from his arms. "Care to help me make our sundaes and we can kick our boots off on the porch?"

The moment of kissing her had passed for now. After holding Polly in his arms, he knew there would be other moments of moonlight or sunlight. It didn't matter. "Lead the way, ma'am."

Her hand slid over his shirtsleeve, and she interlaced her fingers with his. "I'm not sure if you're the real deal, but I kinda hope you are."

5

_P_olly kept her fingers laced with Clint's as they strolled up the wide wooden steps into her cabin. She flicked on the lights as they went, and if he was surprised by how bright the interior of her home became, he never commented. It was one way she chased away the ghosts. Everyone knew they didn't like light. They couldn't wrap around you and take your breath away where there were no shadows.

She pointed to a cupboard. "The bowls are in there and the spoons in the drawer right under it." Soon ice cream containers, sauces, nuts, and the bananas were on the kitchen tabletop. With a snap of her fingers, she said, "Whipped cream."

Clint opened the refrigerator and handed her the red and white can. They fell into an easy conversation about the merits of toppings. Laughing like old friends, it was comfortable and the cloak of worry that had been draped over her shoulders slipped away. She held her bowl, heaping with everything from the table and a generous sprinkle of nuts.

"In case you couldn't guess, I adore banana splits. When you combine the gooey goodness with the banana, it's a balanced treat." With a playful poke in his arm, she said, "How did you know?"

His eyes grew wide. "I did not know, but who doesn't love ice cream?"

They walked through the house, and she toed off her boots by the front door, wiggling her toes in bright-pink ankle socks. "You're welcome to let your toes breathe if you want."

His eyebrow arched. "I'll keep them on tonight, but I appreciate the offer."

Maybe his philosophy was like that line from one of her favorite movies, *Smokey and the Bandit*, when the bandit says he only takes his hat off for one thing. How the heck did her mind swerve to that topic which was so far off the table it wasn't even in the state?

"Polly, are you okay? Your face is flushed."

"Yeah. I'm going in to get a match for the candle. I mean, I have candles, and I'll need to light them so we can see each other." She needed to stop blathering about a match and the candle lest he think she was trying to set a romantic mood. Not that there was anything wrong with that, but, oh jeez, she needed to stop overthinking everything tonight.

He took her bowl and said, "I'll wait for you here."

Thank heavens he seemed to catch on that she needed a minute and maybe he did too. She hurried back to the kitchen and pulled open the junk drawer where she found a book of matches and then, after a few deep calming breaths, she returned to the porch.

Holding them up triumphantly, she announced, "Found them!" She picked up the tall clear glass globe from the fat candle in the middle of the table that sat in front of two cane-backed rocking chairs. Within moments, the candle was glowing softly, and she replaced the globe.

Clint glanced at the house and the candles. "Not a fan of the dark?"

Her heart thudded in her chest. "Why, candles are romantic and we're on a date."

He passed her bowl over, and they settled in the chairs. Polly had lost her taste for the sweet treat, but spooned up a small amount. He had guessed one of her secrets.

From the corner of her eye, she saw him looking straight ahead. Earlier she had promised him to always be truthful and at the first hiccup, she retreated behind a glib comment.

"Actually, I'm not a fan of the dark. It's a long story and I'm not ready to talk about it. Suffice it to say I happily pay my electric bill."

"Good to know. And for the record, I'm a really good *chase the bogeyman away* kind of guy."

His crooked smile and silly comment cut the tension, and she relaxed back into her chair and ate her sundae with gusto.

"What's the best thing about being a working cowboy other than riding horses every day?"

Clint stopped his spoon midway to his mouth and set it back in the bowl. "That is definitely a plus. I guess I like the rhythm of the job and being outside, even in rain or snow. I've been at the ranch since I graduated from community college. Books weren't for me and there's something about working the land that I find satisfying."

"Do you think Annie's idea of the resort is going to help or hurt the ranch?"

He seemed to weigh his answer. "She's a very smart

woman and if she thinks it's the right direction for us, then I have no reason to believe otherwise. Before coming back to the ranch, she had worked evaluating businesses to help them grow."

"I didn't know that." She scraped the bottom of her bowl, slightly embarrassed that she had inhaled her dessert. "Her plans for the gardens and greenhouse are very ambitious, and it's something more ranches should embrace."

"It put a crimp in one of our revenue streams, composting the manure. Now we're using it on the ranch instead of selling it. But again, I'm not one for business plans. I'm the brawn to execute the plan."

She laughed. "I've never heard of anyone refer to themselves as the muscle, except in a gangster movie."

"Do you like the movies?"

She noticed how easily he diverted the conversation to a safe topic. "I love them. I've got a ton of classics on DVD and on rare occasions I'll even go to the movie theater." What she neglected to say was it would be a Sunday matinee, never at night. "What do you like? And if you say westerns, I'd be shocked."

"Actually, I love superhero and science fiction the best. Something about fantasy trips my trigger, but I'm not a huge fan of horror flicks. Most of them are so far out there, using gore as a shock factor, there usually isn't much of a plot."

"Exactly what I say. Give me a classic Alfred Hitchcock and I'm there, but all this other stuff"—she shook her head —"just gratuitous."

Clint set his empty bowl on the table. "Polly, I've had a real nice time tonight and I'm glad you agreed to go out with me."

Her insides went a little mushy as he leaned forward, clasping his hands together. "I've had a great time tonight, too. I'm glad you asked."

"Would you like to do something on Sunday, or is that too soon?"

As she looked into his sable-brown eyes, she knew that the only thing she wanted to do was spend more time with him. "I'd like that. Is there something specific you have in mind?"

"We could take a couple of horses and go for a picnic down by the river, and if you'd like, drop a line and catch supper? We could cook the fish at my place."

"Well, that sounds nice, but there are a couple of issues with that idea." She got up and crossed the porch to sit on the railing. Clint followed her, the soft thud of his steps comforting.

He perched on the railing next to her. "You don't fish or like to eat fish?"

"No, I've got that covered, but I don't ride." The words came out in a rush. "I've never had the opportunity to take lessons."

"You work on a ranch. Anyone would have been happy to give you a few pointers." He held out his hand, and she took it.

"I'll need more than pointers. I've never even come within ten feet of one."

"Would you like to learn? We could start with a lesson after work tomorrow and then, if you want, we can do a brief ride on Sunday. We'll take one of the UTVs out to go fishing if you're not ready for horseback."

She smiled in the growing darkness. "Are you sure it'd be okay with a lesson tomorrow? I've been dying to get on a horse. They're so majestic."

"I've got just the horse for you. When you're done for the day, come find me and I'll let Linc know I'm cutting out early. Just wear comfortable jeans. You're gonna need to be able to put your foot in the stirrup and sit astride the horse."

A nervous laugh escaped her. "Maybe we should start with me petting one and feeding it an apple or carrot."

He gave her hand a light squeeze. "Not to worry, that's part of the lesson." He leaned in closer, and his woodsy cologne teased her senses. "I'll have you riding like you were born in the saddle in no time at all."

"That's a bold promise, sir."

He leaned in and tucked a lock of her hair behind her ear, and his tender touch caused a shiver to race down her arms. She longed to lean into him and let his strength wrap around her, but it was too soon. He needed to know the full truth before she allowed herself to be that vulnerable with him.

He seemed to sense her hesitancy and didn't come any closer. "Time for me to say good night." He stood and pulled her up, too. "Walk me to my truck?" Desire lingered in his eyes, but it comforted her that he didn't act on it, pushing her faster than she was ready to move. Still holding hands, they walked the short distance to his driver's door.

"I had a great time tonight and if you're sure you want to teach me to ride, I'm up for it."

"You work on a ranch, so it makes sense for you to be comfortable in the saddle. Besides, it's a lot of fun. We can go on trail rides, even camp out at night if that's your thing. Sleeping under the stars next to a fire, well, there's nothing like it on earth."

She knew what he meant. Sleeping under the stars had

always been her happy place, well, before, anyway. "I'll make sure I pack an extra apple."

He kissed her forehead in a totally platonic way. "See you tomorrow."

"Good night." She hurried up to the safety of the porch and waited until he backed out of the driveway before blowing out the candle and carrying the bowls in the house, locking the door, and securing the deadbolt behind her. Would there ever come a time when she wasn't looking over her shoulder?

After washing up the dishes, she picked up her phone and dialed her sister.

"Hey, Margo, I hope it's not too late to call?"

"Paulina, this is a pleasant surprise and you can call me anytime, day or night. How's life in big sky country?"

They had agreed never to say where exactly she was living, even though Margo had reassured her Matthew had moved on and was no longer interested in stopping her from living her life. But they both knew he could change his mind at any time.

"All good here. I had a date tonight with a super nice guy."

Polly heard Margo give a whoop of excitement.

"The woman is living again!"

"It was one date, nothing that amazing. It was dinner and a stroll through town." But it had been one of the best nights of her life, even if she was downplaying it to Margo.

"Anyone I know?" She laughed and they both knew that was impossible. Margo hadn't been able to come out and visit yet and it had been two years since they had seen each other. Not because they hadn't wanted to, but Polly felt it wasn't safe.

"Remember I told you about the man I met a few years ago?"

"Dimples?" Margo released a dramatic sigh.

Polly laughed. "Yes." Everything they said was always some kind of code which was dumb, especially since Matthew had said he would take a deal with the courts and was now a free man, supposedly reformed. However, leopards couldn't change their spots, and neither could Matthew.

"If things go well, how about you come out for the holidays this year? It should be safe. I need to live my life again. As far as Matthew is concerned, he got his point across when he asked for the divorce and had me disappear. There's no way I'd ever say a word against him now."

An icy chill filled her heart. At the end, her marriage to Matthew had been filled with worries of unsavory characters and missing money. He had said even law enforcement had gotten involved. When Matthew convinced Polly she needed to leave Portland, it was for her safety and his, and even Margo's. So she had. But she missed her sister.

"I'm sorry you had to go through so much, but for the first time in a few years, I feel like my sister is coming back to me."

"I miss you a lot, Margo. Promise me we'll make plans." Her heart lurched when she thought of all the time that had been lost between them. "And maybe when you come out, I can introduce you to a handsome cowboy or two."

6

---

*T*he next afternoon Clint was in the barn setting out tack. He'd picked Nahla, a gentle mare, for Polly's first riding lesson. His cell phone vibrated in his back pocket. After he withdrew it and glanced at the screen, he couldn't help but smile. It was a text message from Polly, and she wanted to know where to meet him.

He tapped out a text and said he'd meet her in the dining hall in fifteen minutes if she was done for the day. A smiley face and the thumbs-up emoji came back within seconds.

He ran his hand down Nahla's sleek dark neck and leaned close. Talking in her ear, he said, "I'm going to introduce you to Polly. I really like her, so you be extra sweet today and there's an apple and a carrot as a special treat." Her ears twitched as he spoke, and then she nickered softly after he rubbed her velvety nose.

A low chuckle drew his attention to Linc, who was hovering in the wide barn doors.

"So that's how you get around the horses. Promise them extra treats?"

"Hey, man, I didn't hear you come in." Clint wasn't embarrassed to be caught talking to the horse. Most cowboys had a tight bond with their mounts.

"That was obvious." Linc strode toward him. "What's with having Nahla out? Are you going riding?"

"What's with the questions? Can't a cowboy help this little mare stretch her legs?" His smile grew. "But if you need to satisfy your curiosity, I am giving Polly a riding lesson and I thought Nahla would be a perfect mount for her."

"Lesson from beginning to end?" He inclined his head to the saddle stand, blanket, and bridle.

"I believe you have to know how to do it all with the horse, and I hope she enjoys the entire process."

Linc scratched between the horse's ears. "It's been a long time since you put this much effort into anything for a woman." He gave Clint a side-eye. "What is it about this girl that's special?"

Clint ignored the reference to his past and shrugged. "I feel like I know her." He tapped the center of his chest. "I can't explain it, but from that first day she came out here to talk with Annie."

"But you'd seen her around town. What was special about last year?"

Clint glanced at his watch. "I gotta get to the dining hall to meet Polly, but I never saw her around town much. I'd occasionally bump into her at The Trading Post, but never out and about. Besides, she wouldn't even look me in the eye; she always avoided me like the plague or something. I thought she was standoffish."

With a quirk of his brow, Linc asked, "Was there a spark then?"

"I always thought she seemed nice but quiet and yeah, I guess even then there was something I couldn't put my finger on. Even though there was an invisible wall there, it drew me to her, and it wasn't just her beautiful face." He gave Linc a light punch to his shoulder. "I gotta get going. Say hey to Annie for me."

"Will do, and Clint, take it slow and easy with her."

"Will do." He tapped his fingers on the brim of his Stetson. "Wish me luck."

"The woman likes you already, not that I know why." Linc laughed.

Clint pulled open the wooden door to the dining hall and glanced around the large space. It was more than a place to eat three squares a day. There were leather couches, oversized chairs, and a large screen television that dominated the far wall beside the ten eight-foot-long tables with chairs in one section where most of the men gathered. No one bothered to cook in the cabins when Quinn was in the kitchen. What he served was like eating in an excellent restaurant at every meal.

"Clint. Over here." Polly was standing near the beverage station. "Water?" She held up an empty glass.

He walked in her direction, his smile splitting his cheeks. She looked gorgeous in slim-fitting jeans that clung to her curves, a graphic tee that had a picture of a horse and said I'd rather be riding across the front, and on her head a light-blue ball cap with a flower in the middle that must be one of her favorites because of the well-worn look.

"Hi. Polly. You look ready to get started on our adventure." He wanted to lean in and kiss her cheek, but Linc was right. The last thing he wanted to do was spook her.

She pressed a hand to her midsection and said, "I'll confess I'm a little nervous. What if I fall off?"

"You have nothing to be worried about. I've picked out a gentle mare and today you're going to learn how to saddle her. We'll just do some slow, simple walks around the paddock. Then, when you're feeling confident, we'll make plans to take that trail ride I was talking about."

She held out the glass of water to him, and he took it, giving her a smile. "Thanks." After he drained the glass, he held out his hand. "Ready to meet Nahla?"

With a quizzical look, she said, "Is that the name of my horse?"

"It is." He liked how her hand fit perfectly in his as they walked to the exit. "She's about ten years old and she's as gentle as a feather against your skin." He held the door open for her.

"She's still a big animal."

He could hear the quiver in her voice. "I promise you, I won't leave you."

She glanced at him, her large hazel eyes full of trust. A distant memory flashed, but it was gone as quickly as it came. He'd figure out why she seemed so familiar at some point. For today, he was going to enjoy spending time with her.

As they entered the barn, the interior seemed dark compared to the bright sun. Clint steered her down the center of the barn toward Nahla's stall. "I thought I'd bring her out and let you get to know each other, and then I'll show you how to put her bridle on and saddle her up."

"Will she bite when I do that?"

"No. She's very mellow and I'm going to show you the right way, but first you two need to get acquainted."

A soft snort and the sound of hooves shuffling reached his ears. He laughed when Polly's steps slowed. "Don't be nervous. I had a chat with her before and she's a sweetheart."

Polly gave his hand a light squeeze. "I trust you."

Her words were laced with something deeper than just about this riding lesson, as if on a different level she knew he was as steady as the ground beneath their feet. He released her hand and slid back the bolt that held the stall door and it swung open.

He grasped Nahla's halter and guided her out and snapped a lead line on it. She stood next to him, her deep brown eyes seeming to assess the newcomer.

"Polly, this is Nahla." He rubbed the mare's soft nose.

She took a step closer to the horse and tentatively stretched out her hand, her fingers trailing down the length of Nahla's face, from the mare's forelock and ending at her muzzle. She softly snorted and stood still, as if sensing Polly's reticence.

She lifted her gaze to meet Clint's. "I never knew their noses were so soft." She took a step closer and murmured, "Sweet girl, are we going to be friends?"

Nahla gave a snort and shook her head. At first Polly's eyes grew wide and when she noticed he was grinning, she laughed. "I guess that's normal."

"Absolutely. It's important you get acquainted with each other before we begin the next part of your lesson."

He handed her a brush. "Run this over her neck and keep talking to her, just like you were doing. In a few minutes, we'll saddle her up."

"Are you sure we're ready for that? It seems like we need to spend more time like this, just petting her." Her eyes flickered with concern.

"Trust me, we won't rush a thing, and if you get nervous at any time, we'll slow it down. But have faith in yourself, too. You can do this."

She nodded. "It's just so new to me." While she ran the brush over Nahla's neck, Clint watched as the stiffness left her shoulders and her face was bright with a wide smile.

He gave Nahla plenty of time to get used to Polly's touch and soft voice. When it seemed like they were both ready, he said, "Ready to saddle her?"

Polly set the brush down and nodded. "Yes, what do I do first?"

Clint handed her the saddle blanket. "Place this on her back and rest it on the top part near the base of her neck."

She quickly put the blanket on and smoothed it out, and when he handed Polly the saddle, she took a step back at its heft. He reached out a hand to steady her.

"I didn't expect it to be so heavy. But I've got it now." She placed the saddle on her back and moved through cinching the girth belt and finally he handed her the bridle and showed her how to put that on. When she finished, she was beaming.

"Look at me, first time I've ever saddled a horse!"

Handing her the reins, he said, "Let's walk out to the paddock and take one trip around before getting you in the saddle."

He gave her a side-glance. Her face was a mixture of happiness and excitement, without a hint of nerves.

"You say you've never ridden before, not even a pony at a carnival?"

Without looking at him, she said, "I was raised in Chicago."

Now that made sense. She was a city girl. "How did

you end up here? It's not exactly anything like your hometown or Portland."

"I lived in Portland for about fifteen years. Until a few years ago, anyway. I decided a change of pace was in order. Things in my life were complicated, and I needed something… different."

This was about as different as it got, but he didn't press the matter. Her mouth clamped shut, her lips a straight line, and the sparkle that had been in her eyes dimmed. Why she left wasn't any of his business.

They made a slow circle around the paddock and Polly was totally in tune with Nahla, to the exclusion of even talking to Clint. He chuckled to himself. They were quite the trio. Nahla plodding along next to Polly and him on the other side of the pretty woman who was fast capturing his heart.

When they made a full circle, Polly stopped walking, and that sparkle was back in her eyes. "How do I get on her?"

"Well, you've certainly gotten into the spirit of this adventure." He pushed the brim of his hat up. "The city girl might just turn into a country gal."

"I'll have you know I left the city girl behind a long time ago. I'm just catching up to the real me, whoever she might be." She tipped her head. "And it's all going to be thanks to you." She stood on tiptoes and brushed her lips over his cheek. When she took a step back, her cheeks were slightly pink.

"I'm not doing anything other than teaching you to ride."

"Never underestimate the power of a kind gesture, Clint." She averted her eyes and rubbed her hand over Nahla's muzzle.

The statement hung in the air with so many undercurrents he didn't understand what she really meant. This woman was a puzzle, and he was willing to put in the time and see if the pieces of their lives might fit together.

7

*P*olly was sitting in a saddle and she lifted the reins to encourage Nahla to begin the slow journey around the paddock. The rolling motion of her gait was relaxing and exhilarating at the same time. What had ever made her nervous about riding a horse? She glanced at Clint, who was about ten feet from where she was, keeping in line with them.

"If you want to ease into a trot, you can."

Her heart rate kicked up. Could she? "How do I do that?"

"Apply gentle pressure with your calves to her sides and then relax your body as you absorb her movements. Don't get tense in your legs trying to stay still; it's a graceful type of movement. Think of it like walking with a cup of coffee and you don't want to spill it. Relax and enjoy it."

His voice was gentle, and his patience seemed to have no end. She did all that he asked and soon they were trotting. It felt awkward as the dickens, but she was doing it!

"Clint, look!" She turned in the saddle and waved.

Instead of flowing with the trotting motion, she lost her balance. A vise squeezed her chest. In an instant, she had a memory of that day. She must have lost her footing standing at the top and was sliding down the hill, rocks tumbling around her. She closed her eyes and prepared herself to hit the ground. Her blood thundered in her veins, but not from falling off Nahla, then the memory that flashed was gone. Why couldn't she remember more?

With a thud, she landed against Clint's body. "It's okay. I've got you."

Was she really in his arms? Polly opened her eyes and looked into those same soft brown eyes. This was another memory. But no, it was real. The concern on his face overshadowed her own lingering fears. As he helped her stand, he snaked his arm around her waist, giving her support.

"Are you hurt?"

"No. Other than my pride. I guess I got cocky and fell off." She looked over at Nahla, who was patiently standing as if to say what are you doing over there. He still hadn't released her.

"I'm okay, Clint." She gave him a wry smile. "Isn't there a saying, when you fall off, you have to get right back on the horse?" Besides, it was better than getting frustrated that the memory surfaced from the day of her accident, then slipped away.

He tipped his head. "They do. Are you up for that?"

She wiped the palms of her hands on her jeans, stood up straight, and strode to Nahla's side. "Girl, we're going to try this again." She placed her foot in the stirrup, grabbed the saddle horn, and as graceful as possible, swung her leg up and over. "I'm going to stick to walking for the rest of today."

"Make two loops, and then we'll take care of Nahla. If you play your cards right, we can fire up the grill for burgers." A flush moved up his neck, over his cheeks. "That's if you want. No pressure."

"That sounds good, and I can pick some greens and radishes from the garden for salad."

"Workin' together, I like it." He bobbed his head. Again, he kept pace with her as Nahla circled the paddock.

After they had brushed the mare and put the tack away, Polly held out her hand to Clint. They strolled hand in hand down the wide gravel road toward the bunkhouses, where she knew he had a cabin. It was something Annie had filled her in on when she was learning about the workings of the ranch.

"Do you like to cook?" she asked.

"Quinn's better, but I'm good with the grill." He pointed in the garden's direction. "Detour for salad?"

She wasn't in any hurry, so they strolled in the opposite direction toward the main house.

"What do you think about riding? Is it something you'll want to do again?"

With a side-glance, she smiled. "I think so. Despite almost kissing the dirt, I'd like to take a ride with you. Maybe another lesson?"

"How about we skip a formal lesson and pack lunch and ride out to the river on Sunday? We can hang out. It's not a long distance and we can take our time."

She loved being outside. That was one of the reasons she had been drawn to Montana in the first place, the wide-open spaces and miles of hiking trails. Notwithstanding, it was the perfect place to drop off the radar and get away from Matthew. Thinking about him no longer made her look over her shoulder. She was safe as long as she stayed off the grid. She squeezed Clint's hand. Right here and right now was the best place to be for more than one reason.

Over dinner Polly looked out from the small front porch. The sweeping views of the ranch seemed to go on endlessly. "How much land does Annie own?"

Clint pulled his chair close to her so he was looking at the same view and propped his feet on the split-rail porch banister. "Pretty much beyond where the eye can see. Her land goes up into the mountain range. There are some decent caves for exploring. From what Linc said, her parents owned the land next to this. When they died in a plane crash, Pops rolled it all in together, since someday this would all become hers. The house is still there, and she keeps it in good repair, but it's been vacant for years now."

"I wonder if she misses the city. She seems happy here."

He sipped his beer. "Do you miss it?"

She didn't have to think twice. "Not at all. When I left, it was the right thing to do and I've never looked back." What she failed to say was there was still a part of her afraid to go back to what had once been her home. "It's so peaceful here. I don't think I'd ever want to move away from this view."

He took her hand. "That's exactly how I felt when I first stepped on the ranch. Even before I got my cabin, I'd sit out and just look at the view after a long day." He sighed. "But it's a mite better sitting next to you."

She loved the soft drawl in his voice. It touched that tender spot she buried deep in her heart. "I couldn't agree with you more."

Later that night after Polly got home, she prowled around her house. She was surprised and a little disappointed he hadn't pulled her in his arms and kissed the breath from her. But on the other hand, she wasn't sure she was ready for that either. Was she sending mixed messages since she was definitely feeling them? Tomorrow she had to get the house tidy, and she volunteered to pack a lunch for them on Sunday. Tonight, her house seemed empty and she felt alone, almost isolated. It wasn't like people in town weren't friendly, but she had kept her distance from most, always worried someone would ask too many questions and discover she was really Pauline Parker and connect her back to Matthew.

She rubbed her hands over her arms, feeling like someone had just opened the freezer door and she was in danger of tumbling inside. It had been five years of silence from him, and she had not given him any reason to look for her. She had kept her side of the bargain and left him and his life. After double-checking the doors and windows were secured, she wanted to take a hot shower and just go to bed. Her life was getting on a positive track and she would do anything to keep it there.

Polly lay in bed, tossing and turning the events of the day over in her head. The way Clint looked at her tonight and his words played on repeat in her head. *I promise you, I won't leave you.* He said those same words to her as she lay beside the rockslide, broken and bleeding.

She had to tell him. A budding relationship couldn't survive and thrive if it was based on half-truths. It was something Polly had learned the hard way.

Her cell rang, and there was only one person who'd be calling her this late. She picked up and didn't bother checking caller ID.

"Hey, Margo, how did you know I was having trouble sleeping?"

"It's not Margo."

The deep male voice paralyzed her. A thousand thoughts raced through her mind. How did Matthew get her cell number? Surely Margo wouldn't have given it to him.

"Paulina, can you hear me?" His voice commanded a response.

She bolted out of bed and paced the small room. "Matthew, why are you calling me?"

"What? No hello to your favorite ex-husband?" His voice was monotone, and she could picture his face as clearly as if he were standing in front of her.

"You're my only ex-husband. How did you get my number and why are you calling me?" She hoped her voice sounded controlled and mildly interested as she fought the panic that constricted her throat.

"No worries, my dear Paulina. I wanted you to know that the case against me has finally been put in the cold case files. So, you don't need to worry about having to testify against me."

"I told you I'd never do that." The band around her chest tightened, and she fought to maintain control. She breathed in through her nose and out through her mouth, just like her therapist at the rehab clinic taught her when she was going into fight-or-flight mode.

"I know, and I believe you. Have you completely recovered from your fall?"

She dropped to the chair next to the dresser and dropped her head between her knees, still holding the phone to her ear.

"I'm fine." Not that he cared, but she wasn't about to

poke the rattlesnake. Not now. "You didn't say how you got my number?"

"Margo should be more careful with papers she discards. You might mention she should invest in a paper shredder." He coughed. "Your secret location is safe as I promised you, as long as you don't come back to Portland and you maintain your new identity in whatever Podunk town you wound up in."

"How do you know I'm not living in Chicago or another city?" And then it hit her like a sledgehammer connecting to an iron. It was a good thing she was sitting or she would have fallen to the floor. Matthew knew exactly where she was and he had probably always known and what he just said clicked. "You knew about the accident?"

"Paulina, think about that statement. Even though we are no longer married, it doesn't mean I won't continue to look out for you."

She didn't hear a threat in his words, more a reminder she'd never be totally free.

"Now you must tell me. Have you made your mark in flowers like you wanted?"

Idle chitchat was not one of his interests. He didn't really care what her answer would be. She sat up straight on the chair, growing in confidence as if the metal rods in her back were giving her support.

"I'm happy, Matthew." That was all she was willing to tell him. "Please don't feel you need to check in on me again. I'm fine."

"Just do me one favor if you're ever contacted by the authorities. Reach out to me first. I wouldn't want you to have to talk to anyone without a lawyer by your side."

"So now you're offering me an attorney to either take

me down in flames or make sure I toe the line?" She kept the bitterness from her voice. "I thought you said everything was fine."

"It is. But these things have a way of gaining new life."

Those words hit home. The only way it would ever truly be over is when they were all dead.

"Good night, Paulina." The line went silent.

Polly sat in the darkened room, her heart hammering. For a moment, she thought about tossing some clothes in a bag and leaving. Common sense prevailed. If he had known she was here and never bothered to reach out, there was no reason to think it would change. She slipped between the sheets and pulled the covers up to her chin. Sleep wouldn't come easily tonight.

---

8

*C*lint took Polly's front steps two at a time and tapped on her door at ten on the dot. It was a perfect day for a horseback ride and picnic. The wooden door swung inward, and she wore a sunny smile. She unlocked the screen door and pushed it open.

"Hey there." She offered her cheek for a peck. He liked that she was getting more comfortable with him every time they saw each other.

He stepped into the small entranceway. "You look great." She had on light blue jeans and a sleeveless blouse, and her hair was pulled off her face. She looked young and carefree, which made him grin.

"You're not so bad yourself." She pointed in the direction of the kitchen. "I packed lunch, but it needs to stay cool. There's salad, some fried chicken, and fruit with cheese."

"No cookies?" He tried to keep his face neutral, but his teasing tone would give away the truth that he was looking forward to today.

With a playful punch to his shoulder, she said, "Chocolate chip."

He pretended to rub the spot as if it were painful, but in reality, her touch sent his heart racing. What was it about this woman that kept her from wanting to get closer? Clint had to wonder. Did she know he had a weakness for fried chicken?

"Good thing we have a cooler."

Her brow furrowed. "How are you going to strap a cooler to a horse?"

With a chuckle, he said, "It's a cantle cooler bag that's insulated. It rests against the back of the saddle. Picture a saddlebag but made specifically for taking food and drinks on a trail ride. Daphne bought a few to have Annie and Linc try them out before she organizes trail rides for resort guests. I mentioned our plans to Annie, and she asked if we'd give this one a spin."

Her eyes opened a little wider. "Annie knows about our plans?"

"Grace Star Ranch is like a small town where there are no secrets." He tipped his head to the side. "Does that bother you?"

"No." The word came out hesitantly, which made him think she was uncomfortable.

He reached out and touched her arm lightly, not wanting to spook her. "They're not looking for ranch gossip. We're good friends and since they recently got married, they're always ready to give Cupid a helping hand."

As her face relaxed into a warm smile, she said, "I guess having lived in the city for so long, I was pretty much anonymous, and this is a big change; that's all."

"There's always an upside to small-town life too. We

have each other's backs. If someone falls on hard times, a person gets injured, or whatever it might be, folks around here pitch in."

"Sounds a little like Mayberry."

He had never thought River Junction was like the old television show, but he could see how she'd make the connection. "Except we don't have a dorky deputy sheriff always getting into situations that the sheriff has to fix."

"And there's not a freckle-faced, precocious little boy zipping all over town on his bike." She laughed. "I think we've covered the high points of old TV shows. I'll just get the basket and we'll be off."

He headed in the direction of the kitchen and offered, "I'll get it."

She sidestepped, giving him access to the heart of her home, and again, he was pleased to see her comfort level was growing.

Trailing behind him, she picked up a straw cowboy hat on the side counter. "It's right on the table."

He lifted the wicker basket, surprised at the weight to it. "Did you pack every bit of food you had in the house?"

"Ha, you're funny." She set the hat on her head and a saucy smile slipped over her lips. "How do I look?"

Like she wanted to be kissed. He swallowed the lump in his throat but kept a safe distance between them. If there was one thing his momma had said that stuck like a burr, it was *always respect women*. "Like a woman ready to ride a horse."

"Yesterday I was a bit sore, but today I feel great." She stretched her hand out and wiggled her fingers. "I can take that."

"You can get the door." He wanted to get them out of

the small kitchen before his resolve crumbled and he kissed her full pink lips.

A short while later, Clint parked the truck near the horse barn. He was pleased to see Polly didn't just hop out of the truck, but waited for him to open the door for her. With the basket under his arm and her hand in his, they strolled to the barn. A few of the horses stopped grazing and picked up their heads in idle curiosity.

Scanning the paddock, she said, "I don't see Nahla."

"Our mounts are in their stalls. I brought them in before I went to your place. It'll be quicker to get them saddled."

Her steps slowed until she stopped in the bright sun. The brim of her hat shaded her eyes. "Clint, when we were in the kitchen, why didn't you kiss me? I could tell you wanted to."

The direct approach was so refreshing with a woman he was dating, but damn, if it didn't take him aback. "I'm waiting until I'm sure it's something you want."

That sounded lame, but it wasn't like he was about to kiss her and send her running for the hills.

A glint came into her eyes and her hand cupped his cheek, pulling him close to her upturned face. He bent over and waited. He could feel her breath on his face as it quickened. She rose on her toes and tentatively brushed his lips with hers. The pressure of the kiss zinged like an electrical charge through him, and he let her take the lead. Slow and steady, she explored his mouth with soft kisses and nibbles, then she pressed her body against his and wound her arms around his back. In what seemed like seconds, it was over. She stepped back, biting her lower lip as she lifted her eyes to meet his. A twinkle filled hers. "A girl likes to be kissed."

"I can see that now." He stood still, not moving to either walk into the barn or kiss her again. He liked her take-charge ways and wondered what she'd do next.

"The next time you think about kissing me, do it."

He gave one quick nod. "Good to know." He cleared his throat as his heart hammered in his chest. He'd give up riding if she wanted to do more of that.

"Are you going to have me saddle Nahla?"

It was like a snap of a lariat roping a calf. The conversation had veered in a new direction. She took his hand again, and he liked the weight of hers in his as they walked into the barn.

"I am. It's the best way for you to bond with her. But I'll be right with you in case you need help."

"I won't." She grinned. "Well, maybe just a little. But one of these days, I intend to be a pro."

He had no doubt. She was a quick study. "Come on, I'm ready to ride, and I thought we'd head out to one of my favorite spots near the river. The horses will be able to drink and it's near the mountains, so the views are stunning."

"I'd hazard a guess to say there isn't an unpleasant view anywhere in the state."

"Correct statement." He placed the wicker basket Polly had packed on a bale of hay and whistled softly. Nahla and his horse Blaze poked their heads over the stall doors.

Polly cooed as she crossed the space and took the apples Clint handed to her. It was another way for her to reconnect with Nahla, although she was a smart horse and no doubt would remember Polly. And, well, giving Blaze a treat was just fair. What's good for one horse is good for the other.

They made quick work of saddling the horses, and

Clint transferred their lunch to the saddlebags. "You packed enough for eight people."

"I wasn't sure how hungry we'd be and I'd hate to run out."

The woman was definitely full of surprises. He could see the crispiness of the chicken's skin through the container top and everything else looked delicious, but it was the cookies that made him pause. They were huge and he could see there were chock-full of nuts. In his opinion, that was the only way to enjoy a cookie.

They set a slow and easy pace. The sun overhead was high in the sky, but they weren't in any rush. Polly glanced at him and then looked down the path.

"Have you ever been married?"

Blaze was plodding down the trailhead and he wasn't in any rush to get anywhere just like Clint. He had to wonder, where did this question come from? Surely, she knew he hadn't been married, but he answered her anyway.

"No, never married." Taking a page from her book, he continued to look straight ahead. "You?"

A heavy silence fell over them. Which in itself was an answer, but he would not jump to any conclusions. The way she was quiet, maybe she was a widow; that would explain why she moved to town by herself to start over, leaving painful memories behind her.

"Once, but it's been over for a long time. I'm in a good place now."

"Divorced?"

"Over five years."

Her answer was simple, but it was easy to read between the lines. There was more to this story, but he wouldn't press. She'd tell him when she was ready. He wasn't going anywhere. For right now, the moment was almost perfect, especially now that he knew he was welcome to kiss her.

"No kids?"

She shook her head. "No, that turned out to be a blessing."

Again, much was left unsaid, and he wasn't about to push. In time, the truth always came out, and he wasn't one of those guys who was jealous of the past. Heck, as far as he was concerned, he didn't have a jealous bone in his body. Protective, yes. Jealous, no.

"Did you ever want to have kids?"

He wasn't about to tell her his hope for the future unless she asked. But he wanted a few rug rats hanging around the house, doing things that families do, and he wanted to teach his offspring to love the outdoors as much as he did.

Her voice was so faint that if he hadn't been listening closely, he would have missed her next sorrow-laden words. "Yes, I wanted to have a couple, but I don't think I can. At least not anymore."

She forced a bright smile to her face, but it didn't reach her eyes. "Tell me more about the ranch and what's so special about this river. I heard Daphne and Annie talking about some excursions they were going to add for visitors."

Figures Annie and Daphne had been talking about fishing. From what Clint could see, Annie had been right in hiring Daphne to run the guest cottages and activities. So far, she had come up with several ideas that he thought were spot-on.

"It just so happens the Missouri River runs through Grace Star Ranch and has some of the best trout fishing anywhere in the state. Remember that sleazy guy who was coming around when you first started?"

Polly nodded, and now he had her full attention.

"His name was Gasperini, and he wanted to buy the ranch in the worst way. Raze the working part of the ranch and keep just enough to call it one, build a lot of cottages, and basically destroy what Annie's forefathers built with the sweat and toil of their own labor. Once Annie decided she wanted to build some cabins, she pulled Daphne in, and the rest is history."

"I know all of that since I'm also charged with being prepared to grow a lot of the food for guests as well as ranch hands, which is no small feat, but I'm up to the challenge."

"Of course you are; otherwise, Annie wouldn't have hired you. Just like Pops, she has a good instinct for knowing who belongs here and who doesn't. It's kind of a gift."

Her face broke into a wide grin. "Clint, are you saying that I'm considered part of this large eclectic family?"

He cocked a brow. "Well, yeah. How long have you worked here?"

"Over a year now."

"Then yeah, Polly. If it's what you want, there will always be a place for you at the ranch, and that's not just me saying it. It's just how things are around here."

Polly pressed her calves into Nahla's side and they took off at a quick trot. She flashed him a *catch me if you can* smile, encouraging him to let Blaze pick up the pace. She had no idea how things worked around here, and he was going to love showing her all that life offered.

9

They had been riding for about forty minutes when Polly pulled back on the reins to stop Nahla before they reached the edge of the river. Clint had dismounted and flicked Blaze's reins over a tree limb. Taking in the surroundings, she slid off and followed suit.

"It's beautiful here." She took her hat off and shook her ponytail out as the wind teased it. The ends of her hair tickled her bare arms. Clint was watching her with a bemused smile. He took a blanket from behind his saddle and spread it partly in the shade of the tree, yet still in the sun, too.

Why had she brought up the marriage and kid topics? *Because it's important to me. And before I get in too deep, I need to know if we're on the same path. Not that I'm looking to rush anything, but it's best to be upfront about these kinds of things.*

"It sure is breathtaking here."

He glanced at her before moving around to Blaze. "The ranch or Montana in general?"

He took their picnic lunch out of the saddlebag and set it on the blanket.

"Both. I've never lived anyplace that's so small, yet so huge at the same time." She felt it was an inadequate explanation. Small-town living had taken some getting used to and the wide-open spaces seemed never-ending, but she was happy here. Maybe happier than she had ever been before.

"I know what you mean. A few years ago, I was on a hiking kick. Some friends and I spent at least one weekend a month traveling all over the state to try out different trails. I can assure you the views are spectacular every-where I've been."

She relaxed a bit and kept her face neutral. Should she confess to Clint about the first time they met, even though he wouldn't have known it was her, or just let it lie?

"I did a bit of hiking in Montana." She kept her voice casual, like it was an easy breezy conversation despite her heartbeat picking up with the old familiar panicked feeling when she thought about that time in her life.

He sat down and held out his hand to her. "You mentioned that the other night." He tugged her down next to him. "Have you done any hiking around here?"

She focused on unpacking lunch—anything to keep her hands busy. Keeping her voice even, she said, "My last hike was a few years ago at Glacier National Park."

"I've hiked there. In fact, that was quite the trip." He took the water bottle she handed to him.

"Really? What happened?" She knew some of the story and parts he didn't, but she was curious about what he'd say.

"We were on our last night out. I was with three buddies and there had been a rockslide. As we were picking our way around the rubble, we heard someone moaning and found a woman at the bottom of the ravine, partially under a pile of rock. Me and my buddies dug her out, and we sent one guy for help. Out there in the eastern part of the park, cell service is sketchy."

"She was alone?"

He stretched his legs out in front of him and adjusted his hat, tipping it down over his eyes to cut the bright glare from the water. "Yeah, we never found evidence of anyone with her. I think about her from time to time, wondering if she recovered and why was she out there alone. Hiking solo can be dangerous."

"You mean for a woman?"

His head snapped in her direction at the icy tone in her voice. "Man or woman, it can be dangerous. Bears, mountain lions, and a fall can all be catastrophic. I wouldn't go hiking alone."

"I'm sure there are lots of people who do. Maybe she had a good reason for being alone."

He kept his eyes locked on her. "Hey, I really wasn't being a macho jerk. I was genuinely concerned for her."

"Did you stay with her until help came?" These were questions she had wanted to know. The doctor had said she was brought in by medevac, but there were things she had wondered.

"Two of the guys fashioned a gurney of sorts and we got her to the top of the trail. By that time emergency people were there and they got her down to where a helicopter was waiting to take her to the hospital."

"It was risky moving her."

"One of the guys is a paramedic, and he checked her over before we attempted to move her. Getting her out of the ravine saved time. I'd like to think we helped to save her life."

His face had softened, and a faraway look settled on his face.

Her voice was soft. "Thank you."

His brow furrowed as he looked back at her and shifted on the blanket closer to her. "For what?"

Swallowing the lump in her throat, she lifted her face to look him square in the eye. Unflinching, she said, "Thank you for saving my life three years ago."

His mouth gaped open. She could tell he was confused and stunned at the same time. "What are you talking about?"

"The woman at the bottom of the rockslide was me, and if you hadn't found me, I wouldn't be here today." This time, her voice broke. The raw emotions bubbled up and tears formed in her eyes. Wiping them away, she jumped up and walked to the edge of the water. This was not the way she planned to tell Clint her true identity.

She could feel him standing behind her. He wrapped his arms around her, and keeping a small space between them, she leaned back into his body and finally let the tears flow. He didn't speak; he just waited as her body rose and fell. After a while, she said, "I should have told you when we first met. I'm sorry."

"Stop. You have nothing to apologize for. You weren't under any obligation to tell me anything until you were ready."

Polly took a step away from him and turned. "I'd like to tell you the rest of the story. If you'd like to hear it."

He held out his hand. "Let's sit. You can tell me whatever and how much or how little, judgment free, about why you were alone."

Too keyed up to sit, she squeezed his hand. "Can we walk for a bit?"

"Whatever you want."

His voice was gentle, and it wrapped around her heart like a tender hug, giving her the courage to speak. "I came to Montana to try and disappear from my previous life. My ex-husband is not the man I thought he was when we got married. He was and still is into some unsavory stuff. I was being pressured to lie for him or he was going to jail. While we were going through an ugly divorce, my ex kept delaying the final signatures. He kept saying it was complicated and he needed me because a wife can't testify against her husband. For a while I was afraid for my life."

Polly expected Clint to ask what she meant, and she paused, waiting, but he kept his word and waited for her to share what she wanted.

"The people he was laundering money for aren't the most forgiving sort. I knew little at the time of what was going on, but eventually all the pieces fell into place. All I wanted was the divorce. I didn't care about possessions. It was time for me to put distance between us, and surprisingly he agreed to set me up in Nevada in a rental." She stopped walking and said, "Did you know it's not easy to get a divorce in Las Vegas? You have to be a resident for six weeks with the intent to live there permanently."

"I guess getting married there is much easier."

With a snort, she said, "Yeah, you can get stinking drunk and some yahoo will still perform a ceremony. Anyway, I'm getting off topic. I rented a house, got a job at a home improvement store, and planned on staying, but the best-laid plans have a way of going awry. I was able to get the divorce. Those people I mentioned that ex-hubby was in cahoots with, well, they found out where I was and decided I needed to be encouraged to keep my mouth shut; my ex warned me they were coming. Not that I had any intention of saying a word. Instead, I left Nevada and spent my time being a nomad."

"You mean homeless?"

She lifted a shoulder. "I prefer nomad."

"How did you end up on that trail?"

She turned them back in the direction they had come. "I was camping out, living off the grid, not leaving a traceable footprint. Unfortunately, I don't remember. Occasionally, I get snippets of memory, but I remember virtually nothing after sitting by the fire at breakfast. The only logical explanation is I must have been hiking down the trail and stepped on the edge of the rock and it gave way. The next part, you know."

He steered her toward a log under the shade of a river birch tree. "After you got to the hospital, I just couldn't bear the thought of abandoning you. You were all alone with life-threatening injuries. Did you know I came to see you a few times?"

She nodded and looked at the ground. What would he think if she knew it was his stories of River Junction that drew her to the small town? Did it matter? Honesty was the only way they could be friends, or maybe more.

"You would sit by my bed and talk about River Junction and Grace Star Ranch, even the lemonade from the Filler Up Diner." She grinned. "You told me to keep your secret that Maggie's huckleberry pancakes were better than your momma's."

He pulled back and chuckled. "I guess you were listening. I figured you were sleeping every time I came."

"All the meds had me exhausted, so opening my eyes was too much of an effort." She made a circle around her face. "I had to have some plastic surgery to put me back together, then rehab, and I was finally able to reinvent myself as Polly."

"That's not your real name?"

Coming clean, even with the bare minimum of details, was liberating. In for a penny or in for a pound was her dad's motto. She might as well tell him her real name. "Pauline Parker was the woman who went hiking in Glacier National Park, and Polly Carson was discharged from the hospital."

10

*E*verything Polly told him was like a gut punch. He knew there was much more to the story, but what this woman had gone through and she was still smiling, was remarkable. At least now he kind of understood why it always felt as if he knew her because they had met.

"Are you still hiding from your ex and his associates?"

"I was, but Matthew called me a couple of days ago. He's known where I've been for a long time. The good news is the situation has changed, although he won't say specifically how, but he said I should be in the clear." Her voice dropped. "But with Matthew, you never know for sure. I will continue to be cautious."

A thought flared. "Do you think someone was behind your fall? Someone who wanted to make sure you were never able to appear in a courtroom?"

Her face fell before it became a blank expression. He knew it was something she had never given a thought to. "I doubt it. To be honest, I don't know anything and besides, I had been camping for several days in that area. It was just an unfortunate accident."

If he and the guys hadn't come along, she could have died out there alone, injured, subjected to cold temperatures or worse, mountain lions and wolves. Inwardly, he shuddered. He couldn't let her see that flash of fear in him. Clint wanted to be strong for Polly, just as he had that day on the trail. He thought it was a little too convenient. What if there was more to it?

"You don't remember anything more about your accident?"

Polly stood and wandered to the edge of the flattened grass and jammed her hands in her front pockets before she turned to face him. "Nothing. That entire day is blank. Well, except for an occasional flash."

He figured that wasn't unusual for a trauma patient to have near total memory loss. From what he had read, it was the mind's way of protecting her from what had really happened out there. From what he had heard, people usually blocked things out if they couldn't face the truth in situations like hers. "Have you ever felt unsafe in River Junction?"

Slowly, she shook her head, her eyes locked on his. "Not really. I mean, a woman living alone needs to be cautious, but I'm not paranoid, if that's your real question."

He waited. She wasn't giving off vibes. She wanted to be physically closer, and he respected that. "You exude confidence, but after what you went through, hiding, living a solitary existence until you settled here, does lend itself to looking over your shoulder from time to time."

Her shoulders and eyes dropped to study the grass. "You know how the experts say if you run into a black bear to not run but appear larger than you are to fake it out?"

"Yes."

"Well, it's kind of like that. Not the appearing bigger part, but the not running away, never turning your back on the predator. It's kind of how I live my life. I project confidence I don't feel, tell myself I'm a tough chick and that I will never back down."

"Camping by yourself in the wilds of Montana tells me you are a badass woman." He gave her a half grin. "I'd think twice about messing with you. Dang, it took me how long just to work up the nerve to ask you out."

She laughed and looked at him. His insides relaxed as he saw her slow and easy smile gracing her lips. "Good to know that I can intimidate a cowboy."

He stood and in three long strides, he was by her side with open arms, and she stepped into him. Pulling her close, he could smell the wind in her auburn hair, strands of it that had escaped her ponytail teasing his skin. He liked how she fit against his body.

"Be forewarned. It takes a lot to scare me off."

"Noted." She wrapped her arms around his waist and exhaled. Clint hoped Polly felt content in his arms, and maybe even safe. But was there someone still keeping tabs on her, other than her ex-husband? Waiting, in case she still needed to be stopped from sharing what they felt she knew about her past life.

"Your mind is racing, I can tell."

Her soft voice stopped his thoughts from spinning with possibilities of danger. "How's that?"

"Your arms held me tighter and I might need to breathe again."

Immediately, he relaxed. "Sorry. I didn't realize."

Looking into his face, she held up her hands and, using

her index fingers, pushed the corners of his lips upward. "Smile. I'm here and I'm fine."

His voice grew husky. "You've become important to me and knowing more about who you are and our earlier connection reinforces that."

"I get it. Now that you do know, please don't go getting all macho dude on me. Just keep being you so we can continue to enjoy our time together. I don't want my past to intrude on my present or future."

"Our history is what makes us who we are today."

"True." She gave him a look through her dark lashes. "Since I've told you my deepest, darkest secret, tell me about the girl who broke your heart and left you in the single state of mind all these years."

Polly was very perceptive. After sharing her deepest secret, he would tell her all she needed to know. "It's a dull and boring story. Boy meets girl, girl meets a different boy, one who offers her all the shiny things in the world. Then the first boy loses the girl, and he's left with a shattered heart."

"Matters of the heart are rarely that simple." She slipped from the shelter of his body and threaded her fingers with his. "Let's have lunch and afterward, you can bare your soul to me."

Clint allowed himself to be led to the blanket, and he stretched out next to her. The last topic he wanted to talk about was Janice, but she was right. Sharing the past was the best way for them to get to know each other better, but damn, if it wasn't embarrassing. He got dumped at the altar for some guy with a fast Mustang, and not the kind with four legs.

~

*L*eaning with their backs against a tree, Clint and Polly sat close to one another, content after lunch, watching the small ripples in the surface of the river slide by.

"It's so peaceful here." Polly gave him a sidelong glance before returning her attention to the view in front of them. "I know Annie owns the land on the other side too, but how do you get the cattle across the water for grazing?"

"We farm the land to the west and we have enough pastureland to the south. But occasionally a few find their way to the other side. They cross in the shallows and when we figure out where they crossed, we drive them back to this side." He held out his hand, and she slipped hers in it. The way their hands fit together was like a glove and it felt darn good. "That is actually how Renee and Hank from Riverbank Orchard got back together. Cows from his dad's ranch found their way into her orchard after crossing the river. After they trampled her new tree stock, Hank offered to help her replant. In a way, cows are good luck around here."

"Doesn't seem like Renee would agree, but it sounds like it all worked out. She got the guy and her orchard planted."

"Since they got married, Hank is working the land with her. He has a law office in town with limited hours and occasionally lends a hand at his dad's ranch. Ford, his brother, came back home and he's really running the place now."

Polly squeezed his hand. "Tell me about her."

Today against the backdrop of the land, her hazel eyes seem more green than gold. Would it cast a cloud over their date to talk about her? But she had shared some of her past with him, so he took a deep breath and slowly let it out.

"I met Janice on a hiking trip to Yellowstone. I was with friends and she was taking a group on a tour. She was a guide back then." He remembered how she looked that first day. Her straight dark hair was pulled back in a sleek ponytail. Her long toned legs were visible from the hem of her shorts to her bright-pink hiking socks. She looked like an ad for the best-dressed hiker, but there was a no-nonsense air around her. And her confidence swirled around her like an old friend. She knew the area and was excited to share her knowledge with the group.

He felt a gentle poke in his ribs.

"Earth to Clint."

He gave her a sheepish grin. "Sorry, I got lost in the past. But I'll tell you whatever you'd like to know."

"What attracted you to her first?" Polly's face was relaxed and her smile encouraging and genuine.

"Confidence. She owned the tour business, taking people on adventures all over the world. I liked how she was talking to a group of hikers. It sounded like this was their first big hike and she took it all in stride, reviewing where they would go and the type of trail they'd be taking. Me and my buddies were headed in that general direction, and I found myself wanting to go on the hike with them, just to see her in action."

"If she broke your heart, I'm guessing you went on that hike and…" She let the word dangle.

"I did. We had a long-distance relationship for the first six months. She came to River Junction that first winter and fell in love with the ranch and set up a tour business here—fishing mostly."

"She sounds like a real outdoors-woman."

Her gentle voice prodded him forward. "She was. There wasn't anything she didn't get once she set her mind to it." He dropped his head and looked at their inter-twined hands. Janice never liked just being still. She had always wanted to be on the move. "Me included."

"How long were you together?"

"Five years. We were getting married, and I bought a small house in town. We fixed it up, and that's where she was living until after the wedding, and then I'd move in. It was how she wanted it, so I agreed." The words soured as they rolled off his tongue. "Hindsight is twenty-twenty. She didn't want me around since she had met someone else, and he was coming to the area more and more."

"But," she sputtered, "surely someone mentioned something to you."

"He was her new business partner. They were working on taking the business to new heights, she told me. It was good for our future." With a snort, he said, "Turned out, it wasn't good for my future. The morning of the wedding, she asked me to come to the house. When I got there, her suitcases were packed and sitting by the door. He was waiting for her in the car parked in front of our house."

Polly's hand flew to her mouth, and she cried, "No, she broke it off the day you were to be married?"

He bowed his head. "It humiliated me. Janice left me to tell my family and friends. On the upside, we had one hell of a party and I got plastered and stayed that way for a couple of days. Until Linc came to the house and asked me what I was gonna do. Sell the house and move back to the ranch or wallow at the bottom of a bottle."

"Sounds kind of harsh."

He heard the soft rebuke in her statement, and he

didn't bother to defend Linc. It had been the right thing to do. "It's what I needed. After I said I needed to clean the house and sell it, he gave me the news that Pops, Annie's grandfather, was promoting me to assistant ranch manager, reporting to Linc."

With a wrinkled brow, she asked, "I thought he was the foreman?"

"He wasn't comfortable with the word manager, but the reality is, Linc oversees everything and is Annie's right hand."

She sighed. "They go together like bees and wild flowers."

He gave her a sharp look. It sounded like it filled her sigh with longing. Could it be that she wanted something similar in her life?

His heartbeat thumped in his chest. "Do you think you'd ever want that kind of relationship?"

11

*P*olly's heart flipped. She wasn't anywhere near ready to have this kind of discussion with Clint. Even if she had thought about what she wanted for her future. "Doesn't everyone want to be special to another?"

Clint applied gentle pressure to the hand he still held in his. "It's how humans are wired, to want a connection with someone special." His eyes searched hers. "There's no pressure between us. We're still getting to know each other."

"Understood." Suddenly nervous, she withdrew her hand and rose to her feet. "It's getting late. We should get the horses back to the barn, and I need to get home."

"Yeah, I need to check on a few things before the work-week starts tomorrow."

Grateful he didn't try to pick up the conversation about relationships, she packed the cooler bag and folded the blanket they had been sitting on. Within minutes, the saddlebags were repacked, and he held Nahla's bridle while she swung into the saddle. As soon as he was seated on Blaze's back, they moved down the path at a slow walk.

"I had fun today. Thanks for bringing me out here."

"Care to do it again sometime?" He held the reins in his hand as if they were a part of him as she smiled.

"I'd like that. I was wondering, would you like to have dinner at my house one night this week? I love to cook and can make almost anything."

A wide grin appeared on his face. "Lasagna?"

She sat straighter in the saddle. "That happens to be one of my specialties. How about Wednesday?"

"I'll bring dessert."

"You bake?" She couldn't help but add a teasing tone to her question; she guessed he'd pilfer something from Quinn's kitchen.

"No, but Maggie at the Filler Up Diner does. She makes the best pies and cakes, so what do you prefer?"

With a laugh, she said, "Surprise me." She applied pressure to Nahla's sides and she began to trot. This had been the perfect day.

Later that night, after a long, hot soak in the tub, Polly sipped a glass of white wine while sitting on the front porch. She replayed the events of the day. Dating Clint was easy, and even sharing her accident with him hadn't seemed to change a thing. If anything, it helped him open up and share a part of his past. But there was one thing niggling at the back of her mind. Could her accident have been deliberate, and why couldn't she remember what happened?

Closing her eyes, she thought back to that trip. She had been staying out of sight, so was it likely someone from Matthew's circle had found her and wanted to make sure she couldn't make trouble? That was too hard for her to even fathom. But what if there was someone who had hurt her? Why didn't they finish her off? She knew from what the doctor had said, based on the amount of blood lost, that she had been lying there for a while, and it was about two miles from where she had camped. She might have been living on a camping trail, but she never went far from her campsite, so what was she doing out there?

Tonight, she was comforted by the shadows that surrounded her, and the area was silent. At this time of night, most folks were home, not that there was ever much traffic on this part of the street. It was so far from her life in Portland she had to laugh. Matthew would hate it here; there was not a gourmet coffee shop within an hour's drive from River Junction. She had been that way at one time, too. But moving here changed all that. The restlessness she bore evaporated within a week after moving into this house. Her cell pinged with an incoming text and she smiled at the thought of her sister reaching out.

Withdrawing it from her pocket, she frowned. It was a number she didn't recognize. Her mouth went dry as she read the message.

You're safe as long as you keep your mouth shut!

Her fingers shook as she tapped in ten digits and waited while it rang. On the fifth ring, Matthew said, "Paulina, this is a surprise."

"This isn't a social call. Who did you give my number to?"

"Why?" he growled.

"I hate when you answer a question with one of your own." She exhaled and scanned the silent darkness. Was she being watched? "I got a text telling me to keep my mouth shut, and of course, I thought of your situation."

With a dry laugh, he said, "Of course, everything always lands at my feet, good or bad; isn't that right?"

"I left my home and friends because of your dirty dealings, and I haven't seen my sister in years. What you did wasn't my fault. You said me leaving and the divorce were all to keep me out of the line of fire and you said everything was okay. Why would someone text me a warning?"

"For good measure, I'd guess. But you're right; how would someone have your number? Are you sure your sister wouldn't give it out?"

"She would do anything to protect me. That even means not seeing me until things are settled, one way or the other."

"I'll make some calls and see what I can find out, but watch your back. They might have your phone number, but not where you live. I'd like to keep it that way."

Polly thought it was ironic he wanted to keep her safe now, but when they were married, he never gave that a second thought. Other than to agree to the divorce and help her relocate to Nevada.

"Do you have security cameras installed at your new place?"

"No, this is a small town." She didn't mention she had deadbolts on every door and replaced all the window locks.

"Bad things happen in Podunk towns, too. Do yourself a favor and order some online. They're easy to install and use the app on your cell phone. You'll get alerts even when you're not home. Well, that's assuming there is cell service where you're working."

She shifted from foot to foot, thinking that was a good point, not that she would admit it to Matthew. "I'll think about it, and if you do find out anything, will you let me know?"

"Yeah, and for what it's worth." He waited half a second before he said, "I never wanted you to get caught in the crossfire. I should have done a better job protecting you."

His words meant nothing to her now. Perhaps years ago when they were still together, it might have changed things between them. But not now. "You should have thought about that before you got into business with criminals." Her finger hovered over the disconnect button, but before she depressed it, she said softly, "Take care of yourself, Matthew." Then she ended the call.

~

*T*hree days later, security cameras and installation instructions littered her small kitchen table. She had never been one to deal with technology, but now she needed to install these on the front, facing the street, and on the back door, covering the yard, and one on the porch, directed at the front door. Just in case she needed to see if someone could get past the exterior cameras, at least she would have a clear view of the door.

She shuddered just thinking of someone breaking in. A rap on the front door caused her to jump out of the chair. Her heart was pounding as she hurried to look out the front window. It beat faster for a different reason now as she swung the door wide.

"Clint, I didn't know you were coming into town."

A puzzled looked flashed over his face. "We had dinner

plans, remember?" He glanced around the room, and she noticed he had a brown dessert box in his hand.

Damn it, she forgot she promised to cook for him tonight. "I'm sorry, come on in." She closed the door after he was inside and flipped the lock. If he heard the click, he didn't acknowledge it.

"We can do dinner another night." He brushed his lips over hers. "You've been a little distracted the last couple of days. Anything you want to talk about?"

She took the box from his hands and gestured for him to follow her to the kitchen. "I can explain."

He stopped just under the kitchen archway and his eyes went to the boxes on the table. "What's all that?"

"Do you want a beer?"

He pulled out the chair closest to him and sat down, nodding for the beer. To his credit, he waited until they were both sitting down. His eyes probed hers with questions.

"Sunday night I got a text from an unknown number telling me to keep my mouth shut."

He opened his mouth, and she held up a hand. "Hold on. Let me tell you the rest of the story, and if you want to hang around while I get this stuff installed, I can whip us up some dinner."

He took a pull on the brown bottle and set it back down. She appreciated how he respected her request.

"I called my ex-husband to see if he gave out this number since very few people have it. During our conversation, he suggested I install a few cameras for added protection. I hate to admit it, but I thought it was a good idea."

She waved a hand over the papers and hardware on

the table. "This is why I've been distracted and forgot about our dinner."

Clint took her hand. "It's okay. We can eat pie for all I care, but why didn't you tell me what had happened? I would have come right over after work today to get these installed."

"It's not your responsibility to take care of me." She hated the sharpness in her voice. Old habits resurfaced, and she reminded herself Clint wasn't Matthew.

"We're friends and I care about you. And if you've been concerned, I could have asked the sheriff to drive by more often when they made rounds. Make sure no one is lurking around."

"If I was overly worried, I could have done the same." She appreciated he wasn't taking this like a macho man where someone was stepping on his turf. He seemed genuinely concerned, and she now regretted not asking for help or at least telling him what had happened.

"What did your ex say? Does he have any idea who's behind the message?" His voice was steady and low.

"No. He's going to see if he can find out anything and let me know. But if you want, I'd love some help to get these installed before it gets dark. It would probably go faster working together."

"That I can do, but on one condition." A small smile tugged at the corner of his mouth.

"What's that?"

"I get the first slice of pie. I'm starving."

"I'll do you one better. If we get these installed fast, I'll scramble up a few eggs so dinner won't be a total sugar fest."

He stuck his hand out. "Deal."

She took it, and he held hers for an extra minute, causing her to look into his eyes.

"If you ever need me, for anything, call me. I've grown kind of attached to you over the last year or so."

Her heart skipped. "I kind of like spending time with you, too." She stood on tiptoes and kissed him. This time it wasn't a simple brush of lips over lips.

$\mathcal{C}$lint tightened his hands on the steering wheel in a death grip. He kept his cool at Polly's since he didn't want to frighten her, but he was worried. Someone had her cell number, which led him to believe they also knew where she lived. He was more convinced now that her accident hadn't been a simple misstep, but someone had tried to hurt her, or worse. As he drove back to the ranch, he wished she had agreed to come with him. At least out there, plenty of people were around all the time, and he knew Annie would never want her to be in town and vulnerable. At least Polly had agreed to call him should anything cause her to worry tonight. Tomorrow he'd do his best to convince her to reach out to the sheriff so they could keep an eye out for anything that might be suspicious.

Driving down the road to the ranch, he noticed lights on at the main house and was tempted to turn in and just run by Annie the idea of Polly staying in one of the empty cabins for a while. But he changed his mind. Polly would have his head. If there was one thing he already knew about her, she was a strong woman and she'd want an equally strong man standing beside her as she faced the unknown.

After he settled in at his cabin, he grabbed a beer and went out to sit on the front steps. Watching the stars had always been a calming force. Glancing toward the horse barn, he noticed a tall lanky man. That rolling gait was unmistakable. Jed Steele.

He called out. "Jed. Thirsty?"

The man changed direction from the bunkhouse to amble his way and Clint went inside and got a cold one for his buddy. Before he could sit down again, Jed leaned against the railing, thanked him for the beer, and took a long drink.

"I'm surprised to see you out here tonight. I thought you had a date with our pretty gardener." Jed pushed the brim of his hat up and his grin framed a well-trimmed salt-and-pepper mustache.

"We had plans, but they were changed. We'll have dinner tomorrow night." He grew quiet, wondering how Jed would handle the situation he was in. "Can I ask you a question?"

"Ya mean more than one, right?"

Clint knew Jed had a quirky sense of humor, and he needed a serious conversation. "I probably have a few. I could use a bit of advice from someone I trust and know will keep it to himself."

Jed rested his dusty cowboy boot on the step. "I'm listening."

"It's about Polly."

"I figured as much. What's eatin' at you?"

Clint looked Jed straight in the eye. "Turns out I had met her before she started working for Annie. Well, sort of.

Remember me telling you about the woman who was busted up on the trail a few years back? Well, that was her, but I didn't know it till a while ago. She was living on hiking trails by herself, trying to keep a low profile. Her ex had gotten mixed up with some bad characters and she felt safer going her own way."

Jed took a pull on his beer and waited until Clint was ready to continue. He appreciated his buddy's patience.

"She got a text a few days ago reminding her to keep quiet, but she didn't tell me what was happening until I walked in on her trying to get one of those do-it-yourself security systems set up."

Using his bottle, Jed pointed to the mountain range. "Strong woman, to be living on her own out there."

"Tough as they come." He felt the pride well up inside of him. This woman was dating him. "I wanted her to come out to the ranch with me tonight, but she insisted she's fine at her place. I offered to stay, but she declined. She's either confident or obstinate."

"I'd suspect a bit of both. From what I've seen, she can hold her ground and make her way. From what you've said, she's competent to know her strengths and weaknesses, like getting the cameras. And I would guess she won't back down from anything."

"I like this woman and I don't want anything to happen to her. Ever since I learned she was the woman we saved, I can't get that image of her lying in the ravine, broken and bleeding, out of my head."

"Clint, I know you're asking me if you should ride in on Blaze and rescue her like the hero from a movie. She's the first woman you've dated more than twice in years. She's getting under your skin and part of the reason why is her strength. You don't want some clingy kind of a woman who wants to be pampered. Follow her lead, spend time with her, and offer your support, but don't try to control the situation. But if it were me, I'd reach out to Sherriff Blackstone and that will trickle down to the local police. They can keep an eye open just to make sure nothing happens when she's in town. We can spread the word around the ranch, and with the gardens close to the kitchen, you know Quinn would never let anyone near her. He's got a soft spot for her now that she's filling his kitchen with organic vegetables."

That was a true statement. Quinn, the dark and broody chef, had become soft butter in her presence. Jed also had a good point. If he and Polly were spending time together doing things, no one would get through him to her.

He drained the last of his beer. "Good thing you were out wandering tonight."

"It had a purpose. Someone said there were mountain lion tracks near the horse barn after they came in for dinner and I wanted to check it out."

He gave Jed a long look. "And what did you see?"

"Tracks and more than one cat. My guess is juveniles looking to get to the foals—easy pickings compared to a horse."

His gut tightened. Annie was just getting her horse breeding program off the ground with a couple of new arrivals and she purchased four yearlings. This was something Linc and Annie needed to know first thing in the morning. "Everything secure?"

"For tonight, yeah, but we need to let the boss know and add some high-powered electric fencing around that barn. You know how Annie feels about her horses, even more than I'm attached to Tonks."

Clint knew that was saying something. All cowboys

had a strong attachment to their horse. Annie's horses were like her children and she'd spare no expense to protect them. He thought of Polly's cameras. "Might want to install trail cameras on the barns for an added measure of security." If something were to set off a camera, they'd have a better chance of protecting the animals before it was too late.

"Ya gonna talk to Annie and Linc in the morning, or should I?"

"We both should and bounce ideas around to get things secured. Meet me at seven at the main house. They'll be having breakfast, but better to get things rolling right away." Clint stuck out his hand to Jed. "Thanks for the advice and the eagle eye on stuff around here."

"It's my home and I like Polly. I consider her a friend." Jed wandered in the direction of his bunkhouse.

Clint waited until Jed went inside before sending a text to Polly.

I saw a shooting star tonight and thought of you. Sleep well.

He watched the dots appear on the screen as she texted him, and then they stopped. His breath seemed to be lodged in his lungs as he waited for a response, and then the dots appeared again.

Thanks for being you. Looking forward to seeing you tomorrow. XO.

The breath escaped his lungs with relief, and he smiled. The feelings she expressed in her simple text mirrored his own. He didn't want to play the high school game of who got the last word, so he slipped the phone in the pocket of his shirt and took one last look over the darkened landscape. He could feel the danger hanging heavy in the air, and he hoped it was nothing more than the mountain lions. Whatever was headed this way, he'd be ready. If it turned out to be more than a big cat, no one would hurt the people he loved.

~

*E*arly the next morning, after meeting with Linc, Clint put the word out about the mountain lions. He wanted to catch up with Polly before the day got busy. He saw her truck was in her usual spot, but he didn't see her in the gardens. From where he stood, he could see no signs of her at the greenhouse. His next stop was the kitchen. Polly and Quinn, the cook on the ranch, had become good friends, more like siblings really, and he was sure they were talking about gardening in some fashion.

As he rounded the corner of the barn closest to the dining hall, his footsteps slowed. Polly was walking toward the kitchen, but in the shadows, he saw movement. His heartbeat hammered in his chest, and he unclipped his pistol from the holster. He wouldn't shoot unless he had to. It was a juvenile mountain lion. He was surprised to see the big cat out in the daylight. That was unusual, but he must be hungry and looking for easier prey and the shadows of the building were decent cover.

Her boots clomped up the steps onto the back porch, and she pulled open the door. She paused as she held the screen, and he caught her smile as she noticed Clint. She went to come back, and he pointed to the cat lingering in the shadow and the smile faded. To her credit, she didn't scream, but went inside. The door banged behind her and it startled the animal who snarled at Clint before darting the other way, slipping around the side of the barn, headed for the distant tree line. The incident had felt like forever but had really only been minutes.

Quinn appeared from the dining hall with a shotgun in one hand, Polly standing by his side. She scanned the area before she raced to Clint, wrapping her arms around him and holding him tight.

"Was that a mountain lion?" she gasped, her voice breathless.

"Yeah, he was stalking you." He wrapped one arm around her waist and held her close to his chest and he could feel her shudder.

"Would it have attacked me?"

"Come on. Let's get you inside and we can talk. But I'll need to let Linc know what happened. We're going to have to contact Fish and Game. This was a little too close for safety."

Quinn was standing on the porch keeping an eye on them just in case any other creatures were lurking. Clint knew his style. The man might be the silent type, but he was strong and would never back down for anyone or anything.

He acknowledged Quinn. "Thanks for coming out."

The chef nodded in Polly's direction. "She might need lessons on how to handle a pistol since she wanders around by herself a lot."

"No, I'll be fine, really." Polly looked from Quinn to Clint, and her legs began to buckle under her.

He tightened his embrace, wanting nothing more than to always keep her safe. "Nothing or no one will ever get through me to hurt you." He kissed her temple. His voice was low and controlled. "You have my word."

13

olly felt safe in Clint's arms, and the way he said no one would ever hurt her, she knew in her soul that he would do anything to protect her. It made her feel safe and secure. Something she hadn't felt in more years than she'd like to admit.

Quinn held the door as Clint guided her inside the big industrial kitchen. He helped her sit down in a chair, and then she began to shake uncontrollably.

He was by her side, smoothing his rough hand over her hair, murmuring she was safe. He just kept saying it over and over again. Quinn came over and handed her a glass of water.

"Take a sip," he urged. "I'll make you some of that mint tea you like."

She took the glass and saw the water jiggling and she set it down. She didn't need to see her nerves. Feeling them was bad enough. Clint still had his arm around her as he knelt on one knee beside her chair. The concern in his eyes melted her heart. Despite the situation, he was as steady as the mountains outside the front door. Where, she thought, the stupid mountain lion should be looking for a tasty morsel, not on the ranch.

Clint held her tight, and she heard footsteps pounding through the dining hall. Annie and Linc burst into the kitchen, both carrying shotguns, looking as if they were ready to do battle.

Annie's face was pale as she hurried to her. "Are you okay, Polly?"

Clint moved away, and his gaze stayed on her.

"Yeah, just a little shaken is all. I came out early to beat the heat today and was on my way in to get some water. I walked right past the mountain lion and never even saw it." She lifted her eyes to Annie. "I am so sorry to have caused all this fuss."

Annie dragged a chair over and sat next to Polly. "They're excellent at fading into the shadows. Even on trails, you might pass within a foot of them and never know it." She squeezed Polly's hand. "It is troublesome that we've got them coming down to the ranch. Clint told us this morning that Jed found footprints near the horse barn last night."

Annie looked over to where Linc and Clint were deep in conversation as Quinn came out of the kitchen carrying two mugs with curls of steam rising.

"Ladies, tea with a splash of fortification." He gave a nod and then strode over to Linc and Clint. Polly heard him say, "You should have this conversation with the ladies. This concerns everyone on the ranch, not just the two of you."

Clint nodded, and he looked at Polly. His sable-brown eyes glinted with a seriousness she had never seen before. But she understood this was about the ranch and safety of humans and animals alike.

He strode back with Linc and Quinn and dropped down next to Polly. "I wanted to fill Linc in on the situation and figured you didn't need to relive it again so soon. I wasn't trying to shut you out."

"I appreciate that, but Quinn's right. We need to know what's going on. Annie and I aren't the kind of women to let anything stop us while we take care of business. So, what's the plan?"

Clint placed a hand on her shoulder. "For today, you're going to have a ranch hand with you."

She opened her mouth to protest. As if he anticipated what she was about to say, Clint shook his head. "Nonnegotiable. You don't know how to shoot a gun, which means you're unarmed. Not that we expect another daytime visit, but we're erring on the side of extreme caution. Juveniles are still learning how to hunt effectively which we're guessing is why he's lurking here; it's an easier food source."

Linc nodded. "I'm going to head down to the target range and set up an area for you and Daphne to learn how to handle a handgun later this morning."

Polly was glad he mentioned Daphne. "I take it she doesn't know how to shoot?" Was this a good time to confess she had a little experience with handguns?

Annie smiled. "She's a city girl and the only gun she's ever held was a water pistol, and that's not quite the same thing."

Clint gave her a half-crooked smile. "Not to worry, Linc's an outstanding teacher."

A refresher course wasn't a bad idea. Her heart sank a little. "You're not coming?"

"If I can, I'll be there. I need to make sure all the ranch hands know what's going on, and that means I'll be making the rounds to some of the back pastures." He gave her a reassuring smile. "But I'll try to get down there and if you want, we can go back down later this afternoon to get in a bit more practice."

Her insides began to untangle as she exhaled. Everything was going to be okay. "I don't have a gun."

Linc gave Annie a look, and she nodded. "Annie's got a few. She can lend you one short term while you're on the ranch, but Clint will take you into town and help you get one."

Annie asked, "Maybe you can take Daphne with you?"

"I'm going to learn to shoot a gun to kill a mountain lion?" Polly could hear her voice quiver as she looked around the small group in a semicircle around her chair. Unless she was really lucky, she highly doubted that was a simple task, especially as they moved quick.

Clint said, "No, you're going to learn how to shoot a gun in case you need to defend yourself. Our goal will be to get Fish and Game out here to set traps to capture the mountain lions and return them back to where they should be hunting. We don't want anyone in the position to try and kill any sort of animal. However, being defenseless is just asking for trouble. If nothing else, you can shoot a warning shot in the sky for help."

She exhaled with a sigh of relief. She didn't want to have to even think about killing anything. "That makes a lot of sense and knowledge is key to all situations." She stood, unsure if she was ready to start her day, but taking a sip of the now tepid tea, she tasted the mint schnapps and she squeaked out a laugh. "Nice touch, Quinn."

He inclined his head and winked. "Keeping with the theme and all."

Asking no one in particular, Polly said, "So, who's lucky enough to be my babysitter for today?"

Annie hopped up. "That would be me for a while. I need some exercise so you can put me to work, too. Then this afternoon, I'll have Rory take over until Clint is back."

"You know I'm in a fenced-in garden."

Annie smothered a smile. "It's only four feet, mainly to keep out deer and rabbits. Mountain lions been known to jump as high as fifteen feet, so we're still going to be a bit cautious."

She swallowed hard and murmured, "I never had this problem living in Portland."

Clint slung his arm around her shoulders and gave her a squeeze. "This is country living, darlin'. But don't worry, you're safe."

All this talk of shooting guns and the incident of being stalked by a real-life mountain lion was unnerving. "Quinn, any chance I could get a large cup of hot coffee? Herbal tea is tasty, but a shot of caffeine is just what I need to steady me right now."

He smirked. "A shot? You got it, Polly."

With a shake of her head, she said, "An appropriate word choice given our topic of conversation." She laced her hand with Clint's. "But I'm not shooting any animals, right? Just a warning shot to let people know I need help?"

"That's right." He clasped her hand tighter and finally the color was coming back to his face, too. This had taken a lot out of both of them.

After a busy morning weeding with Annie, Polly had made it through her first target practice with Daphne and now they were walking into the main house. Mary had promised them lunch, and she knew from experience she wasn't about to miss any meal prepared by the long-term housekeeper and mother hen to everyone on the ranch.

Polly and Daphne joined Annie and Mary on the back patio where the table was set for four. It was complete with a vase of flowers that Polly guessed came from Mary's part of the garden. She had happily turned over growing most of the vegetables to Polly that were needed for the ranch, which included all she wanted for cooking except for her herbs and some flowers.

Annie looked from Polly to Daphne and back. "So how did it go at the range?"

Daphne jammed a thumb in Polly's direction and grinned. "She's a real Annie Oakley. Quick learner and hit the mark almost every time."

Polly felt the heat rush to her cheeks under Daphne's accolades. "Beginner's luck."

"Me, on the other hand, well, let's just say I can hit the broad side of the barn if it doesn't matter where I need to shoot." She was still smiling and didn't seem to care that she wasn't that great of a shot. "I'd be just as happy having a cowboy around if I need to go out and about until this thing is settled."

Annie nodded. "I'll talk to Linc and see who can be on call for you if you have to go to the construction site. With so much activity, I'm sure it would be an animal-free zone, but getting there could be another story." She handed a pitcher of lemonade to Polly. "I talked to Fish and Game. They'll be out tomorrow with traps and said to be careful in the meantime."

Polly poured her and Daphne a tall glass and she took a sip. It was sweet with a hint of tart, just the way she liked it. "This is good, Mary. Thank you."

She puffed up with the praise and lifted the lid on the

casserole dish in the middle of the table and then, for dramatic effect, folded back the white tea towel over a plate. "I hope you're hungry for lunch. I whipped up some Pork Chili Verde complete with corn tortillas. That should give you stayin' power to get through the rest of the day."

Polly's mouth watered as soon as Mary lifted the lid. No one cooked like Mary and that was saying something since Quinn was a superb cook and she had eaten in some of the best restaurants in Portland when she was married to Matthew. She paused as she scooped some of the pork into a tortilla. Why did she think of her old life? It was shallow and empty when she compared it to her life now —a friendly town to live in, good friends, and her relationship with Clint.

"Hey, Polly, are you going to let us have some too?" Annie's voice jarred her back to the present.

She handed Annie the spoon. "Sorry, I guess the day is catching up to me." Well, really, ever since she had gotten the text from the mystery person, she'd been a little off-kilter.

Annie gave her an understanding smile. "It's not every day you discover a mountain lion was watching you and then you get a 9mm put in your hand and we discover you're a natural. Or did you have practice in your previous life?"

And there it was, her past coming back to haunt her. Matthew had insisted she learn how to handle a gun in the early days of their marriage. He always said it was in case of a home invasion and she needed to be able to protect herself, but she realized, it was really in case his work came after her. And it had.

14

---

*C*lint paced Linc's office. "With mountain lions prowling around, we'll need two pairs of men on watch posted throughout the barns tonight."

Linc sat at his desk, his fingers tented as he let Clint blow off steam. He was really venting about the bigger threat to Polly, but how could he tell Linc what was eating at him? He didn't want to betray her trust, but Linc needed to know, just in case someone came around looking for her. What happened this morning brought reality home. She was vulnerable.

"Clint. Sit down." Linc pointed to the empty chair in front of his desk. "Tell me what's on your mind."

He and Linc had been friends for a long time and if he asked the man for his word not to share the information, he wouldn't. He took his hat off and sagged into the chair. Running his hand through his hair, he gave Linc a long look.

"Polly might be in danger." He looked straight at Linc, who didn't flinch.

"You're not talking about something on four legs." It was a statement, not a question.

"Do I have your word that you won't say anything?"

"Annie and I don't have secrets. We agreed that we'd never keep anything from the other again. If this affects Polly's safety and she spends a good amount of time here, Annie has a right to know. But I can assure you it won't go any further unless Polly says it's okay."

Clint knew Linc's word was his bond, and he trusted his longtime friend with his life. "You can tell Annie. When or if Polly agrees, others should hear what else is going on from her." He toyed with the hat in his hands and finally set it on the desk.

"Do you remember when I went hiking a few years back, and we found that woman at the bottom of the ravine, alone and hurt pretty bad?"

He nodded slowly. "You hung around for a few days at the hospital just to keep an eye on her."

"Turns out that was Polly. She had been living on the hiking trails for a while, alone and basically on the run from her ex-husband's business associates. Seems like he got caught up with the type who wants to make sure no one talks to the law. So, they got a divorce, thinking that would give her the protection she needed. It didn't, so she left everything and came to Montana."

"We certainly have enough wide-open spaces to get lost if you want to. She did this alone?" He gave a low, appreciative whistle. "She's one tough woman."

He sat up a little straighter, proud of the woman he was falling in love with. "It seems she was safe for quite a while, but she got a threatening text, reminding her to stay silent. I helped her put up some cameras over at her place, just so she can keep an eye on things and feel comfortable when she's home."

Linc nodded thoughtfully. "You think someone might trace her to the ranch and potentially come after her here?"

He flung his hands up, annoyed that it sounded like some gangster movie. "Maybe. I don't know. But this morning, watching her completely unaware she was being stalked, it made me think what if it was someone from her past? I'm not with her all the time, and I can't protect her."

"Did she ask for you to be her knight in shining armor?"

"Now you're being a lughead. She believes she can take care of herself, but she doesn't even know how to handle a gun and she doesn't own one."

"Well."

The way Linc drawled out that one word had Clint sitting up straight. "Or can she shoot?"

"She was a little rusty, but that woman has definitely handled a weapon before. She's an excellent shot and was comfortable after just a few minutes. If you don't believe me, take her down to the range yourself and watch her. Damn, she's almost as good as you."

Not to think too well of himself, but he was a good shot —not as good as Linc, but better than some of the ranch hands. "That's actually good to know. I'll make sure she gets a handgun for protection, but do you think we need to give the men a heads-up to keep an eye out for strangers?"

Linc rubbed his hand over the midday stubble on his face. "That's gonna be a bit tough with the construction crews coming and going, and we don't know everyone in town. You're gonna need to talk to Polly and see if she's willing to tell the hands, maybe not all, but Jed, Quinn, and maybe Rory. They can keep an eye open and you know the best set of eagle eyes around is Mary."

Clint knew there were never truer words. Nothing happened on this ranch without Mary knowing about it and she could keep her eyes peeled, especially since Polly spent the majority of her day between the greenhouse and the garden. "I'll talk to her and if she gets all stubborn, I'll do my best to convince her to widen her circle of confidants. Not one of us will judge her, that's for sure."

"Heck, some of our guys right now have pasts that aren't storybook worthy, but they're good men and if they weren't, they wouldn't be on the ranch."

Clint rose to his feet and put his hat back on. "I'll find Polly and I'll let you know what she says."

"I dropped her and Daphne at the house for lunch. Annie wanted to hear all the details of their morning and this way her curiosity was satisfied."

Just as Linc mentioned his wife's name, Clint watched his face soften. "You're a lucky man, Linc. You and Annie are really happy."

"Sometimes she's like a burr under my saddle, but I wouldn't have it any other way. Annie's the love of my life."

He knew exactly what Linc met. Knowing Polly was the woman he helped rescue felt like a second chance.

"Hey, Clint, one question. Why didn't you recognize Polly when Annie hired her?"

He circled his face. "Her injuries were severe and caused her to have some facial reconstruction. There's no way I would have recognized her, and she never spoke when I went to see her. I didn't know she was even listening when I talked to her. I thought she was in a coma. Apparently, me talking about River Junction is what brought her here."

Linc stood up and clapped him on the shoulder. Before Clint left, Linc said, "Are you sure it wasn't the man who brought her, not the talk about a small town which are a dime a dozen across the country?"

As he crossed the driveway to the main house, Clint thought about Linc's parting comment. That was something he hadn't considered, but it made some kind of sense. Before he stepped onto the back porch, he paused, listening to the laughter of the women that drifted to him. Polly might not realize it, but those women considered her a good friend, and they'd stand beside her through whatever might come.

He strolled around the side of the house, and his gaze stopped on Polly. Color was high in her cheeks and her eyes were bright. There was no trace of the scared woman from earlier this morning.

"Ladies." He tipped his hat.

Annie held up a heaping plate of cookies. "Care for a sweet treat, Clint? Mary whipped up these Rustler cookies just this morning."

His mouth watered at the mention of his favorite cookie ever. Chocolate and butterscotch chips, along with coconut, pecans, and raisins, combined with oatmeal. It was a flavor explosion on the tongue. "Don't mind if I do." He smiled at Mary. "Thank you for these."

Mary returned his smile. "After the morning we all had around here, I thought they'd be just the ticket to set things right."

He bent down and kissed her soft, wrinkled cheek. "As

usual, Mary, you're spot-on." When he straightened, he noticed Polly was watching the exchange, and she gave him a flirty wink.

"Polly, are you ready to head back out into the garden? I thought I could spend a little time with you since Rory had to take care of something for Linc."

She looked at Annie before answering. "I'll be fine. I plan on sticking to the greenhouse for the rest of the day."

Not one to be deterred, he said, "Then I'll walk you out."

Daphne gave her a playful poke in the ribs. "This handsome man wants to spend a few minutes with you. I say go for it." She leaned over and whispered in Polly's ear, who laughed as Daphne finished her secret.

"I'll just help clear the table and we can go."

Mary shooed her away from the table. "Nonsense. Annie and Daphne can help. There's nothing like a stroll, long or short, with a handsome cowboy." She fanned herself. "I should know; my late husband was one, and I remember what it was like to be young. There's nothing like it." She gave Polly a flirty wink.

She couldn't help herself, and she gave the older woman a hug around her shoulders. "You're incorrigible, Mary."

She patted Polly's cheek as if she were her granddaughter. She wrapped up two cookies in a paper napkin and handed them to Clint. "Take a cookie for later and share them with your gal."

He tipped his hat again and said, "Ladies," before taking Polly's hand.

He noticed she glanced back over her shoulder.

"They're still watching us."

He chuckled softly. "Of course they are. If I know Mary, she's betting how long it's going to take me to kiss you."

Polly's steps slowed. "Maybe I should have gotten in on that action." She tipped her head to the side and stepped in front of him.

He circled his arm around her waist and pulled her to his chest. "I wanted to do this the moment I saw you sitting at the table, but I thought that might be a tad ungentlemanly."

She slipped her hand behind his neck and pulled him close to her. Her sweet breath caressed his cheek. She whispered, "What are you waiting for, cowboy?"

That was all he needed to hear. He swept his hat off his head and lowered his lips to hers. It didn't matter who was watching them. All he wanted to do was let his lips convey what his heart was feeling.

Standing in the middle of the rows of vegetables, he kissed her until her knees buckled against him. "Polly?" He pulled back and his eyes searched hers.

"Dang." She cupped his cheek. "Where has that kiss been hiding?"

"Waiting for the right time, I guess." He wanted to talk to her about telling a few people, but the words didn't come out, not here and not now. "Any chance you want to go hiking with me this weekend?"

He felt her stiffen and pull back. "I don't think that would be a good idea. The last time didn't turn out so great for me, remember, and with lions and a creep's text?"

Her voice trailed off, and he wanted her to feel safe. "I do, and that's why I think it would be good to recreate moments with happy memories."

He could see she was leery, but then a mischievous

glint came into her eye. "Do you mean like sleeping in the same tent?"

"If you'd like." He brushed his lips over hers, and he could feel the goose bumps pop up on her arm. That was a good sign, he hoped.

"On one condition." His breath quickened as he waited for her to answer.

"We don't go back to the same place. I'm not ready to face that much of the past."

He pulled her to his chest. "We'll face it when you're ready. For now, just call me the luckiest guy around 'cause my girl and I are going away for the weekend."

"I'm your girl?"

15

*C*lint kissed her again and said, "Yeah, if that's okay with you?"

A wave of happiness ran from her head to toes, causing every part of her to want to jump up and down with a big fat *yes, I'm your girl*. But instead, she tipped her head to the side and said, "Sounds nice." She pecked his lips and turned to look at the three ladies, pretending not to watch them from the patio. She gave them a finger flutter and a wide *cat who lapped up the cream* kind of grin.

"I need to get to work, and so do you." She tugged on his hand that held hers. "And you don't need to hang out with me. I'm just fine in the greenhouse and I will shut the door. Unless predators around here now know how to open doors, we're all good."

A worried frown crossed Clint's face. "That's something I'd like to talk to you about."

She cast a look around them but didn't see why he would be so serious. "What's wrong?"

He walked her over to a log bench and sat down with

her. Holding her hands, he looked her in the eyes as her heart pounded. She couldn't imagine what had caused him to grow quiet and look as if the world was about to implode.

"I'm going to apologize first and say I had good intentions. I'm sorry."

"For what?" Her words came out in a slow drawl.

"I told Linc about the text you got."

She pulled her hands away and stuck them in her pockets. She looked over the garden as if it needed her undivided attention. Anger burned in her chest. This was just like Matthew, making decisions for her as if she wasn't capable of handling her own life. She took a deep breath and pushed out the breath through pursed lips.

"I see. You didn't think this was something we should discuss before you shared all the nasty details of my private life?"

"Polly, it wasn't like that. After what happened this morning, I was shaken. If this was last year and the ranch was under normal operations, I wouldn't have given it a second thought as to you being safe here. But with all the construction workers coming and going, someone could get on the ranch and stalk you just like the cougar did this morning."

She could hear the logic in his calm explanation, but it still stung. "I can understand where you're coming from, but I don't need Linc to look at me like I'm a liability and ask me to leave my job."

"He and Annie aren't those kinds of people. They care about everyone who works at the ranch. You've become more than an employee. They consider you a friend and family, too."

"Clint, you know how it's been difficult for me to open up. I'm not mad that they know what is going on because it makes sense. You didn't talk to me first; that's why I'm angry. I would like to have been with you when you told them."

She jabbed him in the shoulder. "You did exactly what my ex would have done. Try to put bubble wrap around the little woman because she couldn't take care of herself, but to your credit, at least you told me what you did. He used to skirt around the truth. Like when I learned how to shoot a gun and he said it was just in case we had a home invasion." With a snort, she added, "Looking back, what he didn't say is our likelihood of being invaded was higher than the average person in my old neighborhood where I grew up."

"That isn't fair. I never said or even implied to Linc or you that you can't take care of yourself, but around here we look out for each other. Being a part of this ranch is like our own community and we take everyone's safety seriously, from animals to people."

That took a bit of the indignant wind from her sails. Taking his hand, she said, "I'm sorry if today has been like the point of a steer horn for you. But I'm careful." She gave him a forced smile. "At least I'll be more aware now since I know there are things skulking in the shadows."

She allowed him to give her a one-armed hug. Not that he was completely forgiven. It was going to take some time for her to cool off. She poked him in the chest and then pointed to herself. "You have to promise me one thing if we're going to keep doing this."

He nodded and waited for her to say what was on her mind.

"The next time you feel the need to talk to a friend about my situation, you either tell me first or, better yet, have me in the same room when it happens. I will not have people talking behind my back." She gave him a hard look. "Does Annie know yet?"

"I don't think so. My guess is you might want to go up to the house if you want to be the one to tell her. And Polly, I think we should tell a few others around here." He held up a hand to stop her from jumping in to protest. "You're around Quinn a lot, and Rory and Jed are on this part of the ranch more often than most of the others. We should give them a heads-up to keep their eyes open, just in case someone comes asking for you." He let that comment dangle for a half a second before continuing. "It's better to be forewarned."

"I doubt that anyone would show up at the ranch."

"Do you want to take that chance?" He leveled his gaze at her. His voice was like granite.

She didn't want to think that anyone would be that brazen to come to the ranch. She figured if someone was watching her, they'd just keep an eye out in town or when she was driving around. Reluctant to think anyone would invade this haven, she nodded. "I'll talk to Annie, Mary, and Daphne. If you think we should tell the others after I get done in the greenhouse, I can bump into them at the dining hall at dinner."

He leaned in and Clint smelled of sunshine, horses, and leather. "I'll make sure they're around, and I'll be with you for moral support."

She gave him a faint smile. One she had to pull up from its hiding spot inside her heart. She didn't want to still be upset with him and most of how she felt had been a knee-jerk reaction from her past. Clint was nothing like Matthew. In fact, other than both being male, that was the end of their similarities.

"I'd like that. Thanks." She rose from the bench. "I'm going to walk back to the main house and then spend the rest of the afternoon gardening. You go back to work, and I'll reach out when I'm ready to go to the dining hall."

His face scrunched up in a scowl. "I should walk with you."

She gave her head one final but firm shake. "Nope. You're going back to work. Linc told us that if we do see any animal to wave our arms over our head and appear larger than we are and that should scare anything away."

He brushed his lips over hers. "Just for the record, it won't scare me."

She put her fingertip under his jaw and tipped his face to hers, where she claimed his mouth. When she was done kissing him, she smiled. "I wasn't worried."

Late in the afternoon, Clint walked into the greenhouse just as Polly was cleaning up the workbench. She was planning an experiment of growing lettuce and a few other things in late fall to see what she could do to extend the fresh salad season.

"Hey, beautiful." He swept her close to his chest and kissed her. "Busy day."

"It was, and you, did you get a lot done?"

"I did, and I made sure to get a message to the guys to meet us in the kitchen. I thought it would be easier without everyone else around, just in case anyone might overhear our conversation."

She tipped his hat off his face and grinned. "You have the prettiest brown eyes, and getting a hold of the guys was thoughtful. Thanks."

He groaned. "Guys' eyes are handsome or devilish but never pretty."

"I'll remember that. Ready to walk down?" She slipped her hand in his and tossed him the keys from the rack. "Lock up for me?"

When Polly and Clint walked into the kitchen through the back door, Quinn was stirring a large pot. Rory was pouring himself a mug of coffee, and Jed was washing his hands. The men looked up when the door banged softly behind Clint.

One by one, they nodded their hellos. Why did these men have to be stereotypical cowboys, short on words and long on head bobs?

Clint said, "Guys, come on over here. Polly needs to talk to you for a minute."

There was no mistaking the seriousness of this situation based on the tone in his voice. Jed dried his hands and Rory took a seat at the rectangular wooden table at the opposite end of the spacious room. Quinn turned the flame down on the pot and joined them.

Clint stuck his hands in his pockets and gave her an encouraging smile, almost as if to say she had the floor.

"Thanks for coming. I know you all heard about this morning and my close call with the mountain lion, but that isn't what I want to talk to you about." Clint's eyes never left her, giving her a boost of courage to continue.

"There's another situation that I'd like your help on, though. The other night I got a text message that was a bit threatening. It wasn't anything specific, but Clint helped me install some cameras around my place and I can check on my house during the day, and they even record movement. The genuine concern is if someone comes out to Grace Star Ranch looking for me." She looked at the three men who were standing stock-still, hanging on her every word. She rocked on her feet, trying to decide how much to tell them.

"A few years ago, I had an accident and after that my looks changed because of my injury. I also changed my name and reinvented myself since it turns out my ex-husband was involved in some stuff that wasn't on the up-and-up. No one from my past should know where I live. So, if someone comes around asking for Paulina or Polly, can you just say you don't know me and then tell me and Clint?"

Jed looked from Clint back to Polly. "One of the construction workers was asking about a Paulina two days ago. I told him I didn't know anyone by that name. He said she was his cousin and he had heard she was working in River Junction and maybe even at the ranch." He shifted from one foot to the other. "I'm sorry, Polly, but I said I didn't know a Paulina, but Polly was our head gardener and told him you lived in town."

Her heart sank, and her gut flipped. "It's okay, Jed. Did you tell him exactly where I live?"

"No. I'd never be specific since you live alone, but that didn't seem to faze him since he said he'd catch up with you here in the next few days."

Clint stepped forward and placed his hands on her shoulders, immediately offering comfort. "Have you seen him since?"

"Yeah, in fact, he was still working when I came up to the dining hall. Want me to go down and see if he's still around?"

Polly put a hand on Clint's arm. "What did he look like?"

Jed thought for a minute before saying, "About six four, thin, muscular, dark hair pulled back into a ponytail, and he had a long, thin scar across his chin."

Oh, this wasn't good. "Matthew is here at Grace Star Ranch."

---

16

*C*lint was following Polly home in his truck. The moment he saw her face go white with what could only be gut-wrenching fear, there was no dissuading him. She said her ex-husband was in town based on the description; the mention of the scar seemed to clinch the deal for her.

He'd guess that if the ex was in town, trouble wasn't far behind. There was no way Clint would let her go home alone. Not that she couldn't handle herself, but she didn't need to be alone. But how much danger would she be in from the ex? That was the question that plagued him now.

Her left blinker came on as she turned into her driveway. Everything looked quiet, but that could be deceiving. He quickly parked the truck and got out, following her up the front steps. Her back was ramrod straight and her face drawn. They didn't speak while she unlocked the door and closed and secured the lock once they were inside.

Polly flicked on a small lamp on the table just inside the door and threw her bag and sweatshirt in the upholstered side chair. "I want to check the video feed for the last twenty-four hours. I've been looking at the feed from time to time during the day, but if Matthew was at the ranch, then he knows where I live and has probably been hanging here after dark." She strode to the kitchen, grabbing her laptop from the side table as she went.

His gut clenched as he followed her. "Makes sense."

She looked at him and ran a finger over his tense jaw. "Relax. I've been down this path before and Matthew has never wanted to hurt me. He had plenty of opportunity when we lived under the same roof."

"It's not him I'm worried about, but why is he here now and who might have followed him?"

"Questions I can't answer, but let's look at the video and I can think."

He liked how she included him in looking at the clips and he had a few ideas of what to do next, but some of that response depended on what they saw.

He pulled out a wooden chair for Polly and it grated over the old linoleum floor. She smiled her thanks, and he took the chair next to hers, pulling it close so he had a good view of the screen and, as an added benefit, they were thigh to thigh.

Tapping the keys, she was adjusting the timestamp on the bottom of the screen to late yesterday afternoon, after they finished the installation. "Here we go."

He leaned closer to the screen, surprised at how clear the footage was. "Listen. This even picks up birds chirping in the trees."

"I'm more interested in people." She stared at the screen, her brow furrowed. "I'm going to fast forward to after you left."

They watched as the camera picked up his taillights as he turned right out of her drive. She moved the slider bar at the bottom of the screen to speed up, and then they watched as a sedan slowed and almost came to a stop in front of her driveway.

"Do you recognize that car?"

She shook her head. "Look, it's leaving." Her finger hovered over the keyboard as if she was going to speed it up again when she pulled away. "Look, the same car is back."

The same car was creeping past once again, and his heart ticked up in his chest. Someone was checking out her house. He glanced at the door as if expecting someone to be outside right now, but that was crazy. If he was a betting man, he'd say his truck alone was a powerful deterrent.

The car moved out of sight again, and Polly exhaled a ragged breath. The tension was thick in the air. He placed his hand over hers and she squeezed.

"Clint." The tremor in her voice matched the one in his gut. Someone was sticking to the shadows but stealthily making their way to the front porch. The man was dressed in a dark hoodie so the camera couldn't catch his face.

"Do you think that's your ex?"

Tipping her head to one side, she said, "It's hard to tell. This person is tall, but without seeing his face or body, I just don't know for sure."

The man on the video stopped and turned his head to a loud bang from the street. A glimpse of his face appeared.

Her voice was low and flat. "That's not Matthew." She hit the pause button.

"Are you sure?"

She pointed to the screen and then slid the bar of the

video back and replayed it again. "Matthew's Italian and is always tanned. His skin soaks up the rays like the desert after it rains. That person is pale."

Getting up, Clint paced the small kitchen. This was bad if there were two people skulking around Polly's place. "Let me sleep on the couch tonight. I don't want you to be here alone until we can talk to the sheriff."

She nodded but didn't speak. Her face was devoid of all expression. Clint dropped to the chair.

"Darlin', talk to me. Tell me what's on your mind."

"I don't get it. I'm not a threat to anyone. I walked away from my entire life and started over." She dropped her head in her hands and groaned. "Besides, I don't know anything."

Clint rubbed her back, hoping it comforted her. He could feel the tension in her shoulders start to wane.

"You don't mind staying tonight?" She didn't lift her head but repositioned herself so that he could pull his chair in front of her.

He brushed her hair off her face and cupped her cheek. "If you weren't going to agree to me staying inside, I'd be in my truck all night and that's not as comfortable."

She forced a smile, but it didn't reach her eyes. "By Jed's description, I thought for sure it would be Matthew we'd see on the video. But do you think that means something has happened to him?"

He wasn't sure how to answer that, but in his experience, shady characters continued to live in the shadows and somehow always got by. Not that he'd say something to upset Polly. "I'm sure he's fine. You never said you thought he was behind the text message you got, so I'm going to surmise there are two different things going on."

She chewed her lower lip, which was something he

had never seen her do before. This was the first time she had been this jumpy around him, too. Even with the mountain lion incident, she had been scared, but this was different.

"I should call Matthew. His number is in my call log and I could see if he's okay and also if he's in town." Her words tumbled out before she took a breath. "Matthew wouldn't hurt me. Maybe whoever is on the video found him and decided to…" Her voice died and she shrugged her shoulders. "I don't know what to think or what to do."

Clint stood and pulled her off the chair and into his arms. Holding her close was the only way he knew to help her feel safe. "I'm sure your ex is fine and he'll turn up tomorrow at the ranch, trying to find you. When he does, you can ask him if he knows there's someone hanging around here."

Polly took a step deeper into his arms and laid her head on his chest. "Will you take me to buy a gun and a gun safe tomorrow? I had one when I lived in Portland and even if I don't ever need it, I'll feel better knowing it's here."

"Yeah, we can do that. After we pick something out, we'll go to the shooting range too."

He could feel her nod as she stayed close against him. His empty stomach picked that moment to protest. She laughed.

"Let's make some dinner and talk about our camping trip."

The mood instantly lifted with the sound of her light laughter. He lowered his lips to her mouth and took his time kissing her. He wasn't about to rush her into a more intimate relationship, but he did his best to convey he wanted her.

She pulled back and looked up at him. "We have separate sleeping bags, right?"

Running his finger over the curve of her cheek and jaw, he said, "Yes, you're in control of everything, as far as that part of our relationship is concerned. I'll take it as slow as you want."

She gave him a side-eye. "Is that a line you used to get a woman horizontal?"

The suspicion in her voice caught him by surprise. "I promise you, it is not a ploy to get anything. I don't play games with anyone, least of all a woman whom I want to be in my life for a very long time."

She blinked once, then again. Her lips parted. In a whisper, she said, "I'm falling for you."

Relief washed over him. Thank heavens he wasn't falling by himself. He didn't move to kiss her, but looked deep into her eyes. "I've already fallen."

She laced her fingers with his and tugged. "Does that mean we've created a new partnership?"

A great belly laugh bubbled up at how she phrased it. "Darlin', partnerships are for business. I'd rather we said we're in a friendship complete with romance, fun, and even a few hurdles."

It was as if a cloud flitted over her face at the last word.

She looked at the floor. "I'm sorry about all of that."

With a gentle touch under her chin, he urged her to look up. "If going through this now means we have smooth sailing later, then let's deal with your ex and whoever else comes along. I've told you, you're not alone anymore. Besides me, you have everyone at the ranch who likes and respects you, and they'd never let anyone harm you."

She shivered, but then thrust her chin up and out. "I'm not afraid, you know."

"I've never said you were. But it's always better to face tough stuff with friends who have your back and I'll be by your side. Consider me backup."

"You really think I can handle Matthew and whoever else might be in River Junction because of him?"

"This from the woman who was living on hiking trails for months. Yeah, I do."

She grimaced. "Look at how that turned out. I took a header and wound up in a hospital." Then her face brightened. "But that led me to you."

"Do me one favor. When we go out this weekend, let's have a calm and boring adventure, well, except for the part that we're together."

Standing on tiptoes, she took off his cowboy hat and placed it on the table. "No promises, Mr. Goodman."

He chuckled. "Tell you what. Go take a shower and I'll rustle us up some dinner."

"All the meat is frozen." She frowned. "That is one thing I miss, pizza delivery."

With a snap of his fingers, he said, "I've got something better. I'll call the diner and ask Maggie to put together two dinners to go, including whatever she's got for dessert, and we can run over and pick it up." He tapped his wrist where a watch might sit. "Ticktock."

"Make sure you get two large lemonades. Maggie's is the best on the planet. Oh, and don't forget to order one for yourself, too."

He couldn't help but laugh again at her cheeky grin as she hurried out of the kitchen. That woman was going to keep him on his toes. Before he could dial, he glanced at the live feed on Polly's laptop and without hesitation, he strode to the front door and pulled it open.

17

*P*olly stepped from the shower and towel dried her hair when the murmur of raised voices reached her. She dressed quickly in jeans and a black tee shirt and hurried into the living room barefoot, with her hair dripping. Standing in the open doorway was Clint. She could barely see around him, but that voice was unmistakable. Matthew.

She pressed up against Clint and stepped in between them. "What are you doing here?" She didn't move to let him come inside. He wasn't welcome.

"Paulina, I had to make sure you were okay." He nodded to the living room. "You won't ask me to come in?"

She weighed her options for a brief moment before nodding. "Don't get comfortable. This is a brief visit."

Clint took a few steps back, but she noticed he never looked away from Matthew and then, for a moment, he scanned the area in front of the house. She had to wonder if someone was lurking outside.

Matthew walked in and took a look around. "Nice

place." He flashed her the smile that used to make her smile in return, but not tonight. "Nothing like our old house."

Sleek and modern had been their home. It was a four-thousand-square-foot, cold, and impersonal house set in an upscale neighborhood. It came complete with a security guard and a gate. Now that she thought about that, if anyone could have broken into their home, they would have had to go to a lot of trouble and be determined. What had Matthew been involved in?

He sat down in a leather chair opposite the floral sofa. Clint waited for her to take a seat before sitting next to her. She wished he'd say something, but he was a man of few words and this situation didn't call for him to say anything. Yet.

Matthew looked from Clint to Polly. "You won't offer me a cold drink?"

She wanted to scream. This was so typical of her ex-husband. "No. This isn't a social call. Clint and I have plans."

Matthew gave Clint a slow once-over, from the toes of his boots to his short dark hair. "The new guy in your life." His voice was flat. "What do you do for work?"

Before Clint could answer, she said, "Why did you go out to Grace Star Ranch, Matthew? And the bigger question is, why are you in town at all?"

"I'm worried about you. Things have gotten a little"—he looked out the front window to the street—"complicated. I needed to make sure you were okay."

Clint's voice was low and laced with restrained anger. "As you can see, Polly is just fine. She has friends and neighbors who are there for her."

"When I was coming up the walk, I noticed you have a

security camera. If this town is so bucolic, why do you need them?"

Clint leaned forward. "For people who show up unexpectedly."

Polly placed a hand on Clint's thigh in an attempt to reassure him this was a brief visit. "Since I got a threatening text message, which I told you about, and you mentioned they were a good idea. I installed the cameras and just last night there was someone lurking outside. Would you happen to know who and why someone was at my home?"

"Right. The cameras." Matthew clasped his hands and looked at the floor. "Anyway, a former colleague of mine thinks you may have a large sum of money that they feel belongs to them."

He freaking threw her under a speeding train. She struggled to keep her voice steady as she asked, "How much money?"

"North of half a mill and south of a few."

She sucked in a breath and didn't attempt to keep the sarcasm from her voice. "Matthew, do I look like I'm sitting on a ton of money?"

He shook his head and gave her that look like she was a child. "People who usually steal money don't flaunt it." He sneered as he looked around. "This place certainly fits that criteria."

She pushed her fist against Clint's thigh, struggling to maintain her composure. "I like my home and this town, so just keep your snide looks and rude comments to yourself."

"Who came with you to town?" Clint's voice cut through the air like a razor.

"No one." Matthew sat up straight in the chair. "Why? Has something happened?"

"Didn't you hear Polly say someone was outside the house last night?" He patted her hand, and she released her fist, suddenly feeling the ache in her fingers. Hopefully that wouldn't leave a mark.

His face had an underlying shade of white. "I thought you were joking."

"No. I'm not sure why he left, but he heard something near the road and took off. When I heard today that you were at the ranch asking for me and we saw the video, I thought it was you."

"If it was, I would tell you. I'd never withhold the truth from you."

A snort escaped her. "Right. Like you've been so forth-coming all the years we were married. I thought you were a legitimate businessperson. Turns out you're in the shady business."

That sounded lame as soon as it left her lips, but her emotions were getting the better of her. She was furious at Matthew for showing up and even more angry for once more feeling like she had to pick up and start over again. "Let's go back and talk about why anyone would think I took cash and..." The words died on her lips. "Was I ever going to be asked to testify? Was that a ruse to get me out of the way?"

"Well..." Matthew gave her a sheepish look. "If there had ever been any proof of anything, I'm sure they would have put pressure on you to testify as to what you knew. But—"

"You lied to me?" She jumped up from the sofa and paced the length of the small room and back. Standing with her hands on her hips, she said, "You took the money. You're the one they should be after, not me. Instead of giving the money back, you've perpetuated this story that maybe I took it? You're nuts and you will clear this up. I don't care if they beat the living hell out of you. It's time you come clean, pay the money back, and I can get back to living my life in paradise."

"Paulina, you make it sound so simple. It's not." He reached for her and she took a step back. His hand fell back by his side.

"I don't care what you have to do, but you will make it that simple and do it tonight. I will not spend another minute looking over my shoulder."

"I don't have the money to give them. I never did."

Dropping to the arm of the sofa, she tucked her feet under the cushion. It was an old habit from when she was a kid, but it seemed to ground her so she could think. "What happened to it?"

"Honestly, I don't know." He shrugged and leaned back in a chair. "I have to find a way to make them see reason, but until I do, you're not safe."

For the first time during the exchange between Matthew and Polly, Clint spoke. "She's safe."

Two words changed everything for her. Here was a man willing to do anything to stand beside her during a very difficult time. Instead of Matthew packing her off to Nevada to get a divorce, then encouraging her to change her name and disappear when things had gotten a little hot, and not from the summer sun.

"Dude, you've got no idea who you're dealing with. These are some laid-back city boys."

Polly watched as Clint's eyebrow arched in mild disgust. She didn't want Matthew to speak to Clint in his usual condescending tone.

She looked at Matthew. Her gaze was unflinching. "Okay, let's hold off on the current situation. I have a question that has been bothering me. When I got hurt on the hiking trail and could have died, is it possible it was some of your acquaintances who helped me down the embankment?" Even just asking the question caused her heart to pound and mouth to go dry. But she had to know.

"Possibly."

Clint's hands became fists resting on his thighs. She slipped off the arm of the sofa and was by his side. Not only did he need her, but more importantly, she needed some of his quiet strength. As if understanding what she needed, he wrapped an arm around her waist and pulled her close to his side.

Her throat constricted as she thought back to that trip. Not having a care in the world, reveling in the thrill of being in Montana, big sky country. Spending her days on short day hikes and nights reclined by a small campfire, watching the stars overhead. It was the first time in her life she had really felt comfortable. Living out of her tent had felt like home. When she had gotten out of the hospital and found this house, again she felt like it was home. To hear Matthew confirm one of her worst fears, that her home was no longer a haven, caused her heart to constrict. Louder than she intended, she demanded, "Don't you feel any remorse, literally setting me up to take the fall for you? What happened to being my husband? The vows we took?" She slammed her fist on the arm of the sofa. "What kind of man are you?"

"I'm sorry. There's no excuse for what I did. That's why I came to see how I could help you now."

"Until those people get their money, they'll keep coming after her." Clint's statement hit home for her.

Matthew's face was grim. "Yes."

"You need to figure this out and take responsibility for what you did. Convince them I don't have their money and I never did."

"It's not that simple." Matthew's voice was flat. "The only way to stop them is to give them money I don't have."

"Do you still have our old house?" The real estate values there had skyrocketed after they moved in and remained high. He had a way to raise more than what he needed. It was a matter of being properly motivated.

"You're suggesting I sell my home?"

That struck a nerve. Matthew was the kind of man who prided himself on possessions—the biggest house, the fancy cars and clothes. It was all about his image. It was hard to realize it had never been about her in their marriage. He probably even saw her like one of his trophies.

"You will contact whoever thinks I have their money and tell them you'll sign over the deed to the house. I'm sure it is worth more than what you owe. They can sell it and keep all the money." She pointed to his shirt pocket. "I'm sure you can contact someone and while you're at it, tell them to call off whoever is in town."

"Paulina, it's not that simple." The whine in his voice was completely out of character for him. Matthew had always portrayed strength and swagger.

Clint turned his head to the front of the house and held up a hand and put his finger to his lips. He then pointed to the window.

"I'm going to take a look. Stay here." He gave Matthew a hard look. "That means you too."

He crossed to the front window and, standing to one

side, peered out. He then crossed to the door and looked over his shoulder at Polly, giving her a reassuring smile. "Be right back." He pulled the door closed behind him as he stepped onto the front porch.

She heard him call out. "Hey!"

Pop! Pop! The sound stilled her heart, and she heard a groan, then what sounded like a chair overturn. Without a thought to who might still be outside, she raced to the door and flung it open.

"Clint." She dropped to the porch floor and turned him over. Blood was soaking his shirt from his right shoulder.

In a hoarse whisper, he said, "Damn good thing they didn't have your aim."

18

*P*olly crawled across the floor and pointed over her shoulder. "Get my phone," she shouted. "And towels."

Clint's pain wasn't enough to cause him to black out, but he'd never been shot before and it hurt like hell. He was bleeding, but it didn't seem that it was a gusher. Thank heavens blood didn't seem to make her squeamish. She placed his head in her lap and pressed her palm to the shoulder in an attempt to stem the blood flow.

He looked up and forced an odd kind of smile. "I really got shot."

"Shush now."

Matthew handed her a towel and she pressed it to his shoulder. With her opposite hand, she dialed her cell phone.

"Annie, Clint was shot, and we need help." She had it on speakerphone so he could hear the conversation.

"Polly, take a breath. Did you call 9-1-1?"

"No, I called you."

He could hear Annie yell for Linc to call the emergency line. "Are you guys safe?"

"Yes, Matthew's here. But we need help. Clint got shot in the shoulder and he's bleeding." She was insistent, but not panicked. He was impressed and figured there was time for a meltdown later.

"Okay, you sit tight and we're on our way. The emergency team will be there soon. Be careful."

Living in town had its advantages, but this was a small town and most of the emergency services were volunteer, so it might take time for people to arrive.

"Clint, sweetheart, help is on the way."

He struggled to sit up, but a wave of nausea hit and he waited for it to pass. "We need to get inside."

She held him down, which was easy since his wound had sapped his strength, but the pain was intense. "We're safe, and if anyone starts shooting at us again, I'll use Matthew as a shield." She kissed his forehead.

He placed a hand over hers and realized if the bullet was four inches to the left, it would have hit him mid-chest and he'd be in a very different situation right now. He forced his eyes open, and those pretty hazel eyes stared down at him. "We won't be able to go camping this weekend."

The look she gave him was tender and a touch funny. "That's what you think. We're going to get you some stitches, an antibiotic, and take off like we planned. I'm looking forward to you cooking for me over a campfire."

He closed his eyes. "Yes, ma'am."

If he had been wearing his Stetson, he would have touched the brim as he spoke.

She groaned. "How could something like this happen in this sweet little town? This was the West, but it wasn't the Wild West anymore. That had been long gone a century ago."

The sounds of a distant siren saved him from reminding her that bad things can happen anywhere. Geography wasn't the relevant factor.

"Paulina, I'm going to take off before the cops show up." Matthew took a couple of steps toward the top of the stairs.

Her voice came out like the crack of a whip. "Move off this porch and I'll find out who's after me and tell them everything. I'll tell them everything I know about your backstabbing, slippery eel impersonation. Now who do you think they'll believe? Me or you?"

He hovered as if weighing his options. An ambulance screeched to a stop along with a fire truck and a sheriff's car in front of her house.

"I'm going to wait over there." He pointed to a bench on the porch.

"You'd best stay where I can see you, too." She continued to caress Clint's face. "We've got company."

This time, he didn't answer, but let the weight of his lids take over.

With a small quiver in her voice, she said, "Clint, please open your eyes."

It took a few moments, but he did as she asked. "I was just listening to you put the fear of the devil in Matthew." He gave her a slight wink. "You really are my girl, you know that?"

"You bet I am." She kissed his forehead again as the emergency personnel hurried up the walk and onto the porch.

Everyone looked familiar, but Polly might not know their names. "We got the whole town here."

Joe, a guy he went to school with, asked her to move back so they could examine him, but he held up his hand. "Polly, stay with me."

She moved from his head, placing it gently on the porch floor, and slid to his side, taking his hand. "I'm right here." She kissed the back of his hand, doing her best to reassure him. Talking in a soft murmur, it relaxed the band around his chest.

A few minutes later, they had cut off his denim shirt and he could see Polly's face. The wound must be ugly.

"Clint, good news, buddy. The bullet appears to have gone straight through, but we're going to get you to the hospital to make sure."

"Polly's coming."

Joe said, "There's no room in the ambulance, but she can meet us there."

Annie and Linc stepped forward. "Clint, don't worry. We'll bring her with us."

He gave a slight nod. They eased Clint onto the gurney and before they could put him into the back of the emergency vehicle, he said, "Linc?"

He was next to him in a flash. "Yeah, Clint. What do you need?"

"Don't leave Polly alone tonight. She needs someone looking out for her."

"I can hear you, Clint. I'll be fine. Besides, I'll be at the hospital with you until you're discharged." She gave Joe a nod and kissed Clint's cheek. "I'll be right behind you."

The ambulance doors closed with a thud and Nina, another friend from town, was riding next to him.

"Hey there, Clint. How are you feeling?" She was checking his pulse and pulled away the towel to put some kind of oversized gauze pad on his shoulder.

"Like someone shot me." He closed his eyes against the harsh lights above him. Sirens whooped as they began to move.

"How did that happen?"

He wasn't sure if Nina was asking questions to keep him talking or if she was trying to get information for Sheriff Blackstone.

"We were sitting in the living room talking and I thought I heard the doorknob rattle. I got up to take a look and as soon as I stepped onto the porch, I heard a *pop*, and then a searing pain shot down my arm. It's some of the worst I've ever felt, and then I hit the floor."

"Any idea who it was?" She wrapped the stethoscope around the back of her neck and jotted down something on her pad.

He wasn't about to tell her what had been going on the last day or so, and especially not who Matthew was. Small-town gossip was the worst, and news of the shooting was already spreading like a wildfire in the dry summer months. He was not about to tinge Polly's reputation with even a hint of wrongdoing.

"I have no idea." The small community hospital was about ten minutes from Polly's place, and he closed his eyes. Maybe he could avoid any more questions until after he saw the doc and talked to Polly. He shuddered to think what might have happened if she had gone out on the porch if he hadn't been with her. A full, involuntary body shake seized him.

"Clint." Nina placed a comforting hand on his arm. "Talk to me. What's going on?"

"I'm okay. It just occurred to me it could have been Polly who got shot."

"I didn't realize you two were serious. I'd heard you

were dating, but I guess the grapevine missed a few details."

"No reason for the whole town to know what's going on in my love life." He opened his eyes. It wouldn't matter if they did. He was happier than he'd been in years.

As if echoing his thoughts, Nina said, "Well, I can tell you this. Everyone who's mentioned it thinks you two make a, and I quote, perfect pair."

He started to chuckle, but groaned instead. "Don't make me laugh."

"Sorry, but I can tell you, that is one lady who was worried about her guy. If you could have seen the look on her face when we were lifting you."

He turned his head to give her his full attention. "What did she do?"

"It's not what she did; it's what she didn't do. The look on her face was fiercely protective. That woman would have sprung into action if you had so much as said ouch."

He thought for a moment. It was bizarre how it took something drastic to really see what was right in front of him the entire time. She might not be ready to proclaim it to the world, especially with Matthew in town and the threat hanging over her. But her feelings ran just as deep as his.

The ambulance came to a stop and the backup beeper kicked on. It was a safe bet they had arrived at the hospital. He knew Linc and Annie would keep her safe while the doc was fixing him up. All he had to do was talk her into coming back to the ranch with him tonight and maybe for the foreseeable future until they sorted this all out.

It seemed like forever until Polly came into the hospital cubicle where Clint had seen the doctor. He was waiting to get an X-ray, just to make sure nothing was left behind from the bullet. Based on the size, the doctor thought it was a 9mm and it was a clean shot, but better to be safe. The minute the curtain pulled back and she was standing next to him, he could see the strain on her face and his blood on her shirt.

"Clint." She bent over the bed and brushed her lips over his. "How's it going?"

"What took so long?" He held up his hand, and she took it.

"I had to talk to the sheriff, and then Linc talked to Matthew. Not that he said much other than he was my ex just making his way through town. Of course, no one was buying what snake oil he was peddling. Sheriff Blackstone asked him to stay in town. That didn't make Matthew happy at all, but I'm relieved. If he's here, Matthew makes a better target than me."

Clint didn't agree with that statement since if what the ex said was true, they still believed she had their money, and they would until they learned the truth.

"Clint, can I ask you something?"

He gave her a half smile. "Anything."

Her brows knitted together. "Did you even think for a second that I took the money?"

With a tug on her hand, he said, "Never even crossed my mind. You might have been slow to warm up to me, but I believe you're the most honest and straightforward person I've ever met." He gave her a wink. "Your ex, on the flip side, well, he's as slippery as they come, and I'm sure we can find a way to rectify this situation as soon as I'm out of this hospital."

Shaking her head, she frowned. "Once you get out of here, you're going to get better, and then I'll figure out a way to get out of this mess. I don't want you getting hurt again because of me."

Polly was amazing. Tonight someone had shot at her house, and she was trying to protect him.

"How about we compromise? We're in this together. You've got my back and I've got yours. It's part of the cowboy code. Loyalty."

She leaned over and whispered in his ear, "Giddy up, cowboy."

19

*P*olly lay awake on the full bed next to Clint. In the early morning sun, she watched his strong, chiseled jaw and deep dimples that had softened as he slept. She had changed from her blood-soaked shirt into a cozy sweatshirt she found in his drawer. Just twenty-four hours ago, she had been stalked by a mountain lion, and then Clint was shot. For all intents, it was probably someone again trying to scare her. But none of that was going to work. She would find out what Matthew did with the money and then get it to whoever was after it. The chips might end up being cow patties for Matthew, but she'd finally be able to look over her shoulder and no one would be watching her. Well, maybe except for Clint.

She ran her finger down his arm, not quite touching. He looked so peaceful and color flushed his cheeks. He rolled onto his back and opened his eyes.

"Hey, darlin'."

A warm feeling passed over her as his deep, low voice said those two words.

A frown slipped over his mouth. "Why aren't you resting?"

"I will once I know you're okay. How's the pain?"

He touched the thick bandage on his shoulder and gave her a forced smile. "Nonexistent." He slipped his hand around the back of her neck, encouraging her to bring her face to his. "I do like waking up next to you."

She brushed her lips over his. "This isn't how I would have guessed we'd spend our first night together. You with a bullet wound and me worried you're going to roll onto your shoulder and start it bleeding again."

"I'm tough. Cowboy. Remember? We don't let something like this slow us down."

"I know, cowboy up and all that. You lost a lot of blood and need to rest and recover, so for today, I'm going to be your nurse and you have to do what I say." She eased off the bed so it wouldn't bend under her weight. "Breakfast will be ready shortly."

He started to push up on his good side when he eased back down. "I think my pain med wore off. Any chance I can get some aspirin or something OTC?"

"I'll get you something stronger."

"No," Clint said sharply.

Surprised, she said, "Clint, don't be a hero and take something to ease the pain. You need to rest."

"I need to be clearheaded. We need to talk about what happened and how we're going to fix this mess so you're safe and your ex goes back to where he belongs."

She hovered in the doorway and knew she was about to tick him off, but she would never let him take the brunt of the rage that someone was obviously hurling at her. "This isn't a discussion we're having. I'll take care of my problem with Matthew. While you were sleeping, I developed a working plan."

He cocked a brow. "Really? Tell me what you've cooked up."

"I'm going to make Matthew tell me how to contact these people. And I'll get one of those phones that can't be traced, a burner phone. Once I make contact, they'll know the truth, and he's going to sign over the house to cover his debts." She wiped her hands together as if she was cleaning them from garden dirt. "Problem solved." If that didn't work, she'd just disappear again. Once she got over leaving Clint, it would be okay. At least she hoped she could survive the heartbreak.

With her arms crossed over her midsection and hip cocked to one side, she asked, "I take it you don't approve?" She didn't think his brow could go higher, but it did.

"These people mean business and if any of the movies I've watched are moderately accurate, they don't care about people. Only the money."

"I know that, which is why the house solves all the problems. It's worth a lot more than what Matthew says he owes them, so they'll make a tidy profit as well." She tapped her chin with her finger. "What do they call that, juice?"

Now he grinned. "Good to hear you can speak the lingo, but you might want to just call it interest. No sense planning on annoying anyone."

She relaxed. He was starting to see she could handle this just like everything else that had come her way.

He patted the bed and then held out his hand when she didn't move. "Five minutes?" he asked.

That was a simple request. She sat down, being careful

not to jostle him, leaning against the dark wood headboard.

"Polly, I'm not sure how to tell you. When we met for the second time last year, things changed for both of us. I don't want you to think I'm rushing anything, but neither of us no longer need to shoulder the burdens of life alone. I recognize you're a strong and independent woman capable of anything you set your mind to."

She released a slow exhale. He understood her better than anyone had, even her sister.

"But," he continued, "that doesn't mean you have to face a mountain lion or anything else alone, and you certainly don't need to protect me. I want to stand with you and support you. Not to diminish your strength, but to add to it. You can draw on me anytime you need to."

She was not going to ask him to step up and be there as she faced down anyone. She couldn't help it; she laughed.

Now he did push himself upright to sit shoulder to shoulder with her and despite beads of sweat popping out over his lip, his brow furrowed as he waited for her to stop laughing.

"I'm not sure if you're laughing at me or if you think I'm sweet."

Placing her hands on either side of his face, she kissed him. "Something struck me as funny."

"Tell me."

"Well, we live in Montana, right?"

"Last time I looked outside." He leaned forward to glance out the bedroom window. "Yup, it's Montana."

"Once upon a time known as part of the Wild West, right?"

"Again, true."

She couldn't resist drawing this out and have a bit of

fun building up to the punch line. "Yesterday I had target practice to protect myself from beasties, right?"

He nodded, waiting patiently for her to get to the funny part. "Well, doesn't this remind you of a gunslinger coming to town, gunning down the hero to get to his actual target, the helpless little woman?"

She could tell the moment it all clicked for him. "It's like we're living in an old western where the good guy gets shot from the bad guys, while the sort of bad guy hides in the shadows."

"In the movies, the bad guy ends up doing the right thing and then runs away." He wiggled his eyebrow, causing her to laugh again. "Any hope of your ex taking off for good once this is all just an unpleasant misunderstanding?"

"Until recently, I hadn't heard from him in five years and it was only to check on me." Suddenly she felt like a dope. He wasn't calling to check on her from the goodness of his heart. Matthew was checking to see if they'd gotten to her and she had already turned them back on him. Coming here had been all about saving his own skin.

She smacked her forehead with a snap. "I've been so stupid." After explaining her theory to Clint, he grew thoughtful.

"How do we turn this around?"

"Not we. Me."

He clasped her hand. The intensity of the jolt that zipped up her arm was surprising.

"Don't shut me out. Right now, it's one against who knows how many and your ex is worthless. Those are terrible odds. Let me stand beside you and cover your back."

Polly wanted to cave and say yes, but she needed to

think clearheaded. "I'm going to get us coffee and breakfast." She kissed his forehead. "I'll be back."

"I don't have any breakfast foods in the fridge."

"Not to worry. I'll run up to the dining hall and Quinn will take care of the rest." She gave him a mock salute. "Stay put."

"Wait, since you're basically doing takeout, there's a thermos next to the door that you can use for coffee and a canvas bag to bring back food."

Relieved they were back on an even and easy keel again, she smiled. "I'll be back soon." She blew a kiss in his direction and walked out onto the front porch, looking right and left just in case her unfriendly cat was hanging around. Once she confirmed the coast was clear, she jogged up the path to the dining hall.

Polly hefted an overfull tote bag from one hand to the other. Quinn had loaded it up with pancakes, scrambled eggs, some fruit, and extra crispy bacon, just the way she liked it. With the thermos of coffee in the bag, they had enough food to hold them through lunch, too. She eased open the door, hoping Clint might have drifted back to sleep.

To her surprise, he was sitting up on the leather sofa with his sock-covered feet propped on the table.

When he saw her, he sat up straight and grinned. "I didn't think you were ever getting back with food. I'm starving."

She didn't react to him being out of bed since she wouldn't want to be coddled. "Quinn made fresh eggs for us and packed everything, so it should still be hot." She set the bag on the coffee table. "Are we eating here?"

"Before we do, can we talk about our weekend plans?" He pulled her down next to him and wrapped his good arm around her. "I don't care what all is going on. I would love to go camping with you and we'll stay on the ranch, so if anything happens, we've got a small army around us."

"Would Annie and Linc mind if we camped on the property?"

He chuckled and nuzzled her neck. "There are thousands of acres out there, all belonging to Annie, and I happen to know the perfect spot where we can go."

Her heartbeat quickened, and she smiled. "If you really want to go camping, we can, but you best not let anything happen to you while we are in the wild."

"Not to worry. We'll take a UTV instead of horses or hiking. That way, it's easy to take our gear."

"Then yes. I'd love for us to go camping this weekend." She tipped her head and decided to astound him with a fun fact. "I read somewhere that Montana has the lowest level of light pollution anywhere in the continental United States. Because of that fact, the stars shine brighter here than anywhere."

"Is that so?" He cupped her cheek. "The stars couldn't compare to the bright light in your eyes."

Her hand flew to her mouth as she actually giggled. "Sometimes you're so corny it's sweet."

"It's your fault. You bring out that side of me."

"I'll bet you say that to all the girls."

His face grew serious. "I was never like this with Janice. We had fun, but what you and I have is easy. I don't feel like I have to be someone you want me to be."

She slipped her arms around him. Her heart ached for the man who had been left at the altar, feeling unworthy of love. "All I ask is for you to be exactly who you are. That's the man I love." She pulled back and looked into his eyes.

"And I want you to stand with me as I confront whoever is out there hunting me."

"Darlin', there is nowhere else I'd rather be."

Clint's word was something she could count on until the end of time. Hopefully, she'd have plenty more when this was all done. A memory flashed. She could see herself running down a trail, looking back over her shoulder. Someone was following her. She ran faster. When she looked behind herself again, the ground shifted and her feet were going out from underneath her and she was falling. As she lay at the bottom of the ravine, she had looked up. Two men were looking down at her.

She squeezed his hands so tight. "Clint. I was chased and left for dead."

20

Ten days later, Clint came out of the bedroom dressed to go camping.

"Polly?"

He entered the kitchen and saw a note lying on the table. *Needed to pick up some things for the weekend. Be back soon. XO.*

He set the note down and noticed their bedrolls were sitting by the door, along with two backpacks and a cooler. He checked inside, but it was empty. She must have gone to the dining hall.

Clint's stomach was in a knot and had been for days, and it wasn't any different as he walked into the empty dining hall. Everyone was either enjoying a day off the ranch or relaxing, but a few hands would be working. He walked through the swinging door into Quinn's sanctuary.

"Morning, Quinn. Have you seen Polly?"

His friend didn't look up from the newspaper. A steaming mug of coffee was at his elbow. "She was in about a half hour ago and said she needed to run home to pick up a few things. I offered to go with her, but she showed me her holster she wore under that chambray shirt she wears all the time. I figured she'd be okay. That woman is smart and coolheaded."

His gut tightened. "She is. I hate that she needs protection, but until we get the guy stalking her, it's the best solution. Besides, she's a grown woman and I believe she'll come through this even stronger."

"Polly would kick butt and not bother taking names. You've got a keeper there."

Clint felt his face break into a smile. "I'm a lucky man."

Quinn gave his full attention to him. "How's the shoulder?"

His hand went to the small bandage under his shirt. "Good. Polly did a great job insisting I stay put this past week and give it time to heal. It was her suggestion to push off our camping adventure by a week."

"She's a smart woman. But I'm worried about her. These last few days she's had a haunted look hovering in her eyes. Anything I can do to help?"

Clint poured himself a mug of coffee and sat down. "My guess is the trauma of the shooting had demons resurfacing from her accident and she asked for time to deal with them. Even though we've been together at my place, she withdrew from conversation. I gave her space to clear her head. She knows I'm here when she's ready to talk about it."

Quinn nodded with understanding. "I figured as much. The man partly responsible for her being on the run shows up and you get shot. It triggered something."

Clint wasn't sure he liked the word trigger, but it was appropriate.

"You haven't heard of anyone showing up here asking about her, have you?"

"No, and I check in with the men as they come in for meals. Nothing since we heard about her ex-husband pretending to work for the construction company."

"We haven't seen anyone on her security cameras either. I know she's eager to get back to her place since she's stayed at my cabin for the last week." He smiled, remembering her sweetness. She had slept on the sofa even when he offered to have her sleep with him, just as friends, nothing more. But he knew lying next to her would have been testing his resolve to take things slow. Everything he knew and wanted to know about her made him want to be with her all the time.

"Man, you've got it bad." Quinn got up and went to slap him on his shoulder and stopped. He grinned. "Like you said before, you're one lucky man."

Clint took his coffee and went out to sit on the wide porch of the dining hall. Long after his coffee was gone, he waited. This had the best view of people coming and going. He noticed billowing clouds of dust were trailing behind a sedan as it drove past the main house and in front of the dining hall. The windows were tinted, so he couldn't see who was in the car. He rose from his chair, ignoring the twinge in his shoulder. He stood on the top step as the car stopped in front of his place. Polly? What the flip was she doing getting out of the passenger seat and what's more, was that her ex driving?

She got out and waved. "Hey, my truck conked out just as I was getting ready to come over. Matthew was driving by and offered to bring me out."

He descended the short set of steps and said, "Where's your bag, darlin'?"

She pointed to the back seat, and he grabbed her small duffel bag before turning to give the ex a long, hard look. Matthew seemed to squirm under the intensity and Clint took small delight in that.

"Thanks for driving Polly out."

"Anything for her." He flashed a perfect smile, the kind you saw on dental commercials.

This guy annoyed Clint, but there was something more, kind of the moment before you heard the rattle on a snake, but sensed it was there, anyway.

It took a lot for him to force out a congenial thanks. "Appreciate ya. Now if you don't mind, Polly and I have someplace to be." He slung his arm around her shoulders and pulled her close to his side. He felt better having his body between them.

She placed a hand on his chest. "Thank you, Matthew. We'll catch up next week to finalize the plan to get me out of the line of fire."

"Sure thing, Paulina. You two have a good weekend." He got in the car without a backward glance, turned around, and headed back down the driveway.

Clint wasn't in any hurry to move up to the house. He watched the car and made a note of the license plate number. It had a Washington State license plate, but he got the feeling it was either borrowed or rented.

He noticed Polly kept her eyes trained on the back of the car, too. "I was glad he came by when I needed a ride, but I forgot how odd he is." She inched closer and kissed his cheek. "I'm so glad you're a normal guy." She gave him a nudge to get him walking up the steps.

"What do you mean?" He dropped her bag on the porch floor and took a seat on the bench, pulling her into his lap.

"For an ex-husband, he sure had a lot of questions about how serious we were. If I thought we'd get married and have kids." She pushed back her hair and gave him a warm kiss on the mouth.

"What did you tell him?" His arms tightened around her waist. He liked how she smelled of sunshine and the earth even when she hadn't been in the garden.

Cocking her head, she grinned. "At first I told him it was none of his business, but then I relented and said you made me very happy, but we weren't rushing into anything. We had plenty of time to talk about the future."

"What did he think about that?"

"Just that he thought you were good for me and I looked happier than he'd ever seen me."

He smiled, and she poked his cheeks where his dimples would appear. "And what did you say to that?"

"It's hard to not agree when he's right. I'm happier than I've ever been."

"Even when you were married to him?" He hated that he sounded like a jealous boyfriend, but she had made the statement about being happy. What had her life been like? His stomach turned if she was about to tell him they dined out at fancy restaurants and things he could never give her living in River Junction.

"He worked a lot. He always said it was not the right time to have a baby. I even went off birth control and tried to get pregnant. I figured once I was expecting, he'd be thrilled. But it never happened, so I concluded I can't have kids." She eased off his lap and sat on the porch rail. "Would that be a game changer if we decided to go down that path and we couldn't have a baby?"

Without hesitation, he shook his head. "If I had you in my life, that would be all I'd ever need."

She frowned. "Are you being honest with both of us? Most every guy I've ever met said that someday they'd like a son to carry on his name. And you said your dad wanted a grandson."

"I'm not some men, Polly." She had her arms wrapped around her midsection, and he knew enough to give her some space. Right now, they needed to use their words to have this conversation. There would be time enough for Clint to show her how he felt tonight when they were under the never-ending stars.

Tears slipped down her cheeks, and her hands covered her face. In a flash, he pulled her into his arms. There were no questions now. He could wait until she was ready to talk about what was breaking her heart.

For several long minutes, he held her. His heart broke for the hurt she was feeling. He kissed her hair and ran his hand over her back, all while making soft, soothing sounds. When the tears had slowed, the sound of hiccups replaced them. That too, he could wait out.

"I had a big fancy house in Portland. We socialized with all the right people, as Matthew called them, but I was lonely. I never felt like I was home until I found that little cabin in town. When I started to work for Annie, it was as if I had been reborn."

He had to wonder if now was the time to talk about what she had remembered from her accident.

Almost as if she read his mind, she said, "I know you've wanted to talk about the memory I had when I got hurt and I needed to process it first. But in a way, those men did me a favor. I met you and found where I belong."

"Well, the moment I saw you talking to Annie about her ideas to expand the garden, it was all over for me. You were the most beautiful woman I had ever seen. It was like I had been waiting for you to show up."

She looked up, her cheeks stained and her eyes red from the tears. "Guess looking at me now is a mite different."

"Yes, you're still the most beautiful woman I've ever met, and you always will be."

She wiped her cheeks on her shirtsleeve. "I really appreciate you giving me the space to work through everything the last few days. I'm sure it was hard for you, but I needed the time to do it. I had to put the trauma in the past, and it might rear up from time to time, but eventually it will just be a footnote in my life."

He wrapped his arms around her again and kissed her forehead. She might think it was in the past, but whoever did that to her was still out there. In order for her to live a long and happy life, he was going to find the ones responsible and they would pay. He'd make sure of that.

~

Settled under a blanket next to the fire, Clint and Polly were wrapped in each other's arms. A small pup tent was close by, but it was the stars overhead that had left her speechless. He couldn't help but smile as the coyotes in the distance howled, and she snuggled closer.

He nuzzled her neck and whispered in her ear, "We're perfectly safe, you know."

"The coyotes add to the old-time ambiance. Do you think this is what it was like when people came west? Did they stop and look up at the stars, just like we're doing now?"

To hear the awe and wonder in her voice warmed him all the way to his toes. If he hadn't known better, he would have sworn she was a country girl. "If they didn't look up, they were fools."

Pulling the wool blanket closer around her shoulders, he asked, "If you're cold, I can add more wood to the fire."

"No." Her breath warmed his skin. "I can think of another way to stay warm." The firelight reflected in her eyes and he could see the mischief and invitation there.

"Oh, I think that can be arranged." His mouth claimed hers.

21

The following Thursday, after the camping adventure with Clint, Polly was standing next to her kitchen table, studying the chart in front of her. She had listed all the possible groups from their past of people who might be after her—well, really Matthew. But none of it made any sense. These weren't people from the country club set. Besides he sold luxury boats. If it was cars, she could see people boosting them and selling parts on the black market. But you couldn't dismantle a boat sitting at a dock and sell its parts, could you?

She crossed the cozy room to fix a cup of tea and then glanced at the clock. Clint would be over soon for the long overdue lasagna. She put the kettle on and checked the casserole. The sauce was bubbling, and it looked good. The fragrant aroma caused her mouth to water in anticipation of all that gooey cheese and savory sausage. All that was left was the bread and salad, and of course, the wine. A sharp rap on her front door had her glance at the security app on her phone.

"What the heck is he doing here?" She padded to the

door barefoot and pulled it open. "Matthew, this is unexpected."

He came in before she had the chance to tell him this wasn't a good time. She pushed down the instant flair of her temper. After all, they were in this mess together and she needed to remain civil until it was over, and then the ties to him would be severed.

His eyes widened. "Are you making lasagna?" He patted his midsection. "Good thing I came hungry."

"Dinner isn't for you, and you're not invited."

The corners of his mouth dipped and his eyes narrowed. "No need to get snippy."

Once again, she fought to control her temper. She had always hated it when he said she was snippy—such an old-fashioned term—and she knew he was really calling her the *B* word.

She never moved from the front entrance. "What can I help you with?"

He bobbed his head in the direction of the living room. "Can't we sit? I think I have some news that might help us."

"Ten minutes. I need to get ready."

He gave her the once-over, which at one time had given her a rush of pleasure, but now it was just, well, inappropriate. They were divorced, and she knew it was for the best for both of them.

She waved him into the living room, but she didn't sit. Standing next to the small wood stove, she crossed her arms. He was looking far too pleased with himself to not have something to share. Maybe this wouldn't be a waste of her time.

"Tell me what you have learned."

Rubbing his hands together, he gave her a tight smile,

and a shiver raced down her back. Unsure why, she forced herself to think positive.

"Remember you told me about someone being on your porch the night before Clint got shot?"

Thinking back over the last few weeks, she didn't remember telling him about that person. But maybe she had. Letting it go, she said, "Yes. The person in the hoodie."

"That's the one. Well, it turns out from a reliable source that I think he's a gun for hire, not one who has a grudge against you. I'm guessing after he shot Clint and realized his mistake, he took off. So, for now, you're worry free."

Looking out the front window, she thought about his statement. That someone had been hired to come here and try to scare, or worse, hurt her. That made little sense. From what she had seen in the movies, the bad guys show up and demand what they believe they have coming to them and then, if you don't comply, they threaten you with bodily harm.

Without looking at him, she asked, "Does that mean you're leaving too?"

"Nah, I thought I'd hang around just to make sure everything was okay, and I want to get to know the new man in your life. I need to make sure he treats you right."

She clapped her hands together, and her laugh was dry. "That's rich. You wouldn't know the difference between treating your partner well or not. At least you didn't for the last four years of our marriage."

Giving her a sly wink, he grinned. "The first year was awesome though. Am I right?"

"Matthew, a physical relationship, no matter how intense, doesn't make a long-lasting marriage. I spent more time alone than with you, except for when you needed me on your arm at social events."

"I was working to provide you with a lifestyle you deserved." He got up from the sofa and took her arm, applying pressure. "You never complained about the fancy dinners, spa retreats, the nice cars, or the house we lived in. You just went along for the ride."

She winced and tried to step away, but he wouldn't let go. "You're hurting me." That shiver from earlier came back, this time accompanied by the urge to get him out of the house.

Instantly, he released her, and his face softened. "I'm sorry, Paulina. I didn't mean to cause you any discomfort. The pressure cooker we've been in for the last few years is getting to me. And for some of that time, I didn't even know where you were, if you were safe or, worse, dead."

The words rang hollow as Matthew talked. Rubbing her hand over where his had just been, she looked at the door, wishing Matthew would leave. The only way to do that was to finish this conversation.

"If you think the person who shot Clint left town, maybe you should head home and if something comes up, I'll let you know. It's only a ten-hour drive or a quick flight if you need to come back."

He smiled. "I'm going to stay. Even if you don't want me to get to know your cowboy, you have quick access to me to brainstorm, which could be beneficial. But I have no intention of selling my house, so we'll need to come up with another plan to get that money back to these people."

She gave him a side-eye. What he had said didn't make any sense. "Matthew, if you were in business with them, why don't you know who to reach out to and make it right?"

"Baby, don't you think I tried that years ago? When we first decided you should move to Nevada."

"I'm not your baby anymore, so don't call me that again. And if you had tried, why didn't it work?"

He turned to pace the room and said, "Paulina, it wasn't that easy."

Matthew's explanation was interrupted when the front door opened and Clint strode in. He looked from Polly to Matthew and his face was devoid of all expression. "I heard voices."

Walking at a moderate pace so as not to make it seem like she was worried about anything, she crossed the room and gave him a peck on the lips.

"You're early." She hoped Clint would realize it wasn't an accusation, but he was a welcome sight. "Dinner is still about thirty minutes away."

He handed her a bottle of wine but still kept an untrusting eye on Matthew. "I got done early and there's no place I'd rather be."

Matthew crossed the room with his hand outstretched. "Good to see you, cowboy. The last time I saw you, you were lying on the porch floor, not looking so hot."

"Still strong enough to kick your butt to the curb if necessary." The threat in his voice was veiled, but it was there all the same.

With a laugh, Matthew shook Clint's hand and patted Polly's cheek. "I'll take off, but we'll catch up in a few days, or before if I hear anything else." He walked out the still open door with a tuneless whistle floating on the breeze.

Clint wrapped his arms around her. "Are you alright? I

was a bit surprised when I saw his car out front. I was concerned he might be upsetting you."

"I'm fine. Matthew dropped by with what he thinks is good news about the person who shot you."

His brow shot up. "Oh? Like he knows who it was?"

She looked at the bottle of wine and noticed it was one of her favorites. He really was the sweetest guy. "Not that good. But Matthew thinks since the perp didn't get the right result, he's probably left town to go back to where he came from." She wandered into the kitchen with Clint a step behind her. "Or maybe the whole thing was a setup to scare me and shooting you just took it up an extra notch."

He walked around the room and took a look at the poster board on the table. "What's all this?"

"A whodunit board." She grinned. "Like on those mystery shows I watch, they always have a whiteboard or something where they put the clues. It helps the detectives to figure out who the bad guy is. I thought if I made notes, it might help us find out who Matthew owes and we can wrap this up soon."

She set the wine bottle aside and was standing next to Clint as she pointed to the columns.

"Business partner is where I started. Not that I know if Matthew even has a partner. I added in a loan shark. Maybe he has a gambling problem I never knew about. He does love horse racing. Next, I thought about someone who jacks cars to sell parts on the black market. He sells boats, so maybe it's a possibility. The only other choice is someone has been blackmailing him and this has nothing to do with missing money, but coming after his wife was another way to put pressure on him."

He held his arm out away from his body, a space where she fit perfectly. "You're not married to him anymore."

She stepped into the crook of his arm. "I know that. He knows that. But whoever this is might not know that we're no longer married and I've found happiness with you." She tipped her head back, inviting him to kiss her. After he thoroughly kissed her, she said, "But there is one thing I need your help with."

"Anything. Name it."

"Don't get upset when I have to spend time with my ex-husband. All I want to do is get this behind us so that we can start our future."

"I thought we already were?" He lifted her so her feet no longer touched the floor and twirled her around the room, all the while kissing her mouth, neck, and any other exposed skin he could find.

She was laughing and kissing him until he set her down. "You're right, but I'd like to have Matthew go home and leave us alone."

"How about we agree that I'm around when you and your ex are brainstorming. Who knows? Maybe an outsider's point of view could help speed things up." He nibbled behind her ear and she laughed softly as her insides turned to melted butter.

"I'd never turn down your help as long as you promise to not get jealous if he uses an old pet name or something."

He splayed a hand over his chest. "He let you go, and we found each other. There is not a jealous bone in my body. However, he needs to respect where you are in life now, and if he doesn't, well then, I'll explain how things are. Trust me, he'll get the point."

He ran a hand down her back and frowned as he looked around the room. "Darlin', where's your holster?"

"I locked it up when I got home." She knew where

Clint was going with his question. It hadn't dawned on her until now. Technically, she had protection close by, but if that hadn't been Matthew on her doorstep, it could have been anyone and with her gun locked in the safe, she was unprotected. She placed a hand on his chest and could feel his heart thumping. "If I'm alone, I'll have it on me."

"Just until this is resolved. No sense taking any more chances." He took her hand and kissed the palm, sending another round of shivers down her back, but they were most definitely pleasant.

The timer when off on the stove. In a deep, husky voice, he asked, "Can dinner wait?"

---

he next morning, Clint rode out across the pasture. He had stopped to see Polly in the garden before he headed out, and he was excited to see she was harvesting zucchinis today. With any luck, maybe there would be a bread coming out of either the dining hall, Mary's, or even Polly's kitchen. If it came right down to it, he'd whip up one. Most of them were going to pickles according to Quinn and those, too, would be tasty come next winter.

He thought about Matthew's visit to Polly last night and something didn't sit right. Not that he was a big mystery book reader, but he believed if a thug had been paid to do a job, they didn't make a mistake and then walk away. Unless Polly was right—maybe it was about scaring her.

He rubbed his hand over his chin. With the streetlight illuminating her porch, whoever it was would have seen it wasn't a woman who came out the door. Unless they mistook him for the ex. They were a similar height and body type. He nudged the horse into a trot and headed to ride the fence line. It was a job he liked to do periodically. It gave him time to think.

A few hours later, Clint still felt like some bit of information was just out of his reach. But he did not know what it might be. He kept coming back to the same conclusion that either they were trying to shoot the ex or it was a simple warning. Headed back to the ranch, he moved in the direction of the construction site. Maybe he'd talk to Jessie, the supervisor, to see if there was anyone who hadn't shown up the last few days. How was it that the shooter had known where to find Polly?

Clint took Blaze to a watering trough and looped the bridle around a hitching post. He'd only be a few minutes, and then he'd take his horse back to the paddock.

In the midday sun, most of the crew were reclining and having lunch under the trees that dotted the jobsite. He spotted Jesse next to a pickup truck, talking to a worker. He lifted his hand in greeting as Clint made his way across the dirt.

Jesse extended his hand. "Clint, this is a surprise. I haven't seen you since we were down at The Lucky Bucket a few months back. I heard you're dating that pretty gardener, Polly."

"I am." Clint liked a man with a hearty handshake and since he and Jesse went back quite a few years, he didn't mind the question about his dating status with Polly. "Good to see you."

He gestured to the jobsite. "The framing's going up fast."

Jesse's gaze looked over the entire site, beaming. Could he see it completed? Is that what made him smile? "We've got a good crew that works well together. So that helps."

Just the opening Clint needed. "Has this group been together long?"

"It's our fifth major job. My talent pool ranges from experienced to master artisan." He sounded like a dad talking about his son hitting a home run in minor league. Pride was in his voice and on his face.

"No one new for this job?" Clint hoped he sounded casual, but Jesse gave him a sharp look.

"What's going on?" He leaned against the truck fender. "You seem pretty interested to know about the men."

He trusted Jesse, so he dropped his voice so that it wouldn't carry. "Polly got a threatening text. I guess you didn't hear, but I was shot a couple of weeks ago when I was at her place. I just want to make sure that there isn't someone lurking around here. You know, we're doing all we can to keep her safe."

He nodded. "Hey, man, I'm really sorry. I hadn't heard about you. I was on vacation last week. This is my first day back. As far as I know, we only had one transient worker, and he didn't last long. Matt something. He didn't know a saw from a hammer, and then he stopped showing up after two days. No great loss."

Clint nodded. That sounded like the ex. "Will you let me know if someone comes around looking for work?"

"Yeah, of course, and I'll keep my ears open too. If I hear anything, I'll let you know right away."

He shook Jesse's hand and thanked him. They talked about catching up for a beer one night at the Bucket before Jesse had to get back to work. Clint watched as the men all switched back into work mode and they seemed to all know each other as they laughed and joked around like old friends.

After Clint got back to his office in the dining hall,

something struck him. How could the ex not know the difference between basic tools? With a few clicks on the keyboard, he started researching Polly's old life in hopes something would spark a new idea.

He got lost in his research and notes, and before long, shadows were slipping across the floor. His stomach grumbled. It had been three hours. Each time he thought he had a lead, it went down to a dead end. The internet trail had the ex looking like a choirboy. But you don't reach almost forty without so much as a ticket. So what was this guy hiding?

The sound of boots on the wooden floor heading to his office made him smile. It was Polly's walk. He walked around his desk and perched on it until she entered the small office.

"Hey, cowboy. Hard day on the range?" She closed the distance between them and ran her fingers through his hat-matted hair before dropping a kiss on his mouth.

"Wasn't too bad. Fence looks good, and I swung by the construction site. All is well there, too."

She cocked a brow. "What did you find out?"

He pulled her close and looked into her pretty gold-flecked hazel eyes. "What makes you think I was searching for anything?"

She tapped the end of his nose with her finger. "Because I've been dying to go down there. I didn't have a good excuse and I don't know anyone, so I'd look out of place. Besides, if there is someone working there that has been watching me, it would only reinforce they got under my skin."

A small smile graced her lips, and he brushed her hair off her face. "You've got me pegged. I know the supervisor. We're old friends and his name is Jesse. He's a local guy, grew up a few miles outside of town, actually near Riverbank Orchards."

She nodded. "I know where that is. Go on."

"Jesse said that everyone had been working together for years except one guy who only lasted two days."

Shaking her head, her smile dipped. "Let me guess. Matthew, right?"

He nodded. "You want to hear how Jesse described him?"

"When you set it up that way, yes."

Clint liked how Polly felt in his arms. Warm and soft, but her confidence was very attractive, too. "He said, and I quote, 'the guy didn't know a hammer from a saw.'"

Polly hooted. "Sounds like Jesse had his number. Matthew never did anything around the house. Even if he wanted a picture hung, his idea of doing the work was dialing the handyman. I swear that man was able to start a hefty college fund for his kids on what Matthew paid him."

She eased out of his arms and moved around the desk, plopping down in his desk chair. "I hope you don't mind, but my feet are tired."

"See those papers in front of you?"

She picked up the pad he had been using and scanned his notes. "This is all about Portland?" She looked up. "Why are you looking into my past?"

"It's more about your ex. Something's bugging me and I can't put my finger on it. Yet."

"Um, it's called the typical ex-husband and new boyfriend syndrome. Matthew might be a lot of things—lazy, inconsiderate, and loud—but he's transparent. What you see is what you get."

"If that's true, then why does he appear squeaky clean?"

She wrinkled her nose as her frown grew. "What do you mean? He's far from an angel."

He pointed to the pad. "Read that and tell me if that jibes with the person you know."

She flipped through the pages and looked up. "I'm going to need a large mug of coffee and maybe a cookie if Quinn's got any hiding in the bread box."

"There's a bread box?" How on earth did she know about Quinn's stash when it took him years to find out? He chuckled as he left the office. The chef certainly did have a soft spot for Polly. It was a good thing she fell for him before she really got to know Quinn. With his model good looks and the fact that he really could cook, well, it was a wonder Quinn didn't have women falling at his feet.

When he returned, Polly was still reading the notes on Matthew. Clint watched her face run through a range of expressions. He wasn't sure if she was annoyed that he had spent so much time poking his nose into her old life, well, while she lived there and after she moved to Nevada. Or if she was impressed by the depth of his research. It still didn't give Clint any better idea on what was happening.

A little while later, she put the pad aside as she ate the last of the oatmeal cookie and wiped the crumbs into the garbage can before she met his gaze. "You're right. He's so clean it's like he's the Teflon man."

Clint slapped his hand on his thigh. "That's what I thought. Everyone leaves a trace, a parking ticket or something."

She leaned forward and clasped her hands on the desktop. "Trust me. Matthew is not perfect. He's gotten into a few bar fights in his day and speeding tickets. Well, he's had more than his share. But he paid them and moved on." She leaned back in the chair and looked at the ceiling. "That only leaves one answer. Matthew is caught up with thugs and it's just like he said. They think I took off with their money and now they're trying to scare me so I'll pay off the big boys when they roll into town."

A part of Clint thought that might be the case, but he had a shred of doubt, too. It was too perfect the way it all wrapped up back to money the ex owed someone. However, there wasn't another explanation.

"Polly, as much as I can't stand the guy, maybe you should ask him to meet us at your place tomorrow around seven. We can dig a little deeper into these unhappy loan sharks and thugs. The only genuine hope of getting the heat off you and back where it belongs is to uncover the truth, and unfortunately for us both, the only person who knows is your ex." His gut churned just thinking of that guy anywhere near Polly. It was the only way he knew to trip the guy up.

"I'll call him, but on one condition." She narrowed her eyes. "And you're not going to like it, but hear me out."

"I'm listening." He took a deep breath and exhaled. Her brain had gone into overdrive, and he was sure it wasn't something he wanted to hear.

"I'll ask Matthew to come over, but you have to stay out of sight. You can be in the bedroom or kitchen, but the only way he'll really be candid is if he thinks we're alone." She winked. "You intimidate him."

She was right about two things. He didn't like it, but he was pleased to hear the ex wasn't a fan of his either.

"On one condition of mine. You have your gun on you at all times. I'd hate for any of his acquaintances to come calling and it takes me a few precious seconds to get to your side."

She walked around the desk and slipped her arms around his waist. "Agreed. After all, I am a better shot than you."

Before he could come back with a sharp rebuttal, she pulled his mouth to hers and silenced him with a searing kiss.

23

*P*olly wiped her damp palms on her jeans. Matthew was due any minute, and Clint had just stepped into her bedroom. He was sitting behind the door, where he could hear everything that was said. She had to find a way to get Matthew to open up like he had when they were married.

A tap, tap on the door caused her to look at the bedroom door before moving to the front. She forced a smile to her face and pulled open the door.

"Hi, Matthew. Thanks for coming over."

He leaned forward, and she offered her cheek as he brushed it with his lips. "Always happy to stop by." He glanced around the room. "Where's your cowboy?" His smile grew wider as he realized they were alone.

"He had some things to do, but I'll see him later." She was hoping her voice came off as easy breezy since Matthew was a master at reading her.

"How's his shoulder?" He shrugged off his leather coat and draped it over the chair closest to the sofa.

"He's feeling good, no pain."

"Glad to hear it. If that person had been a better shot, he might not be here today."

That caused a chill to flow through her veins. "But they weren't, and he's fine." She sat down on the chair and he took the sofa, which was perfect since he had his back to the bedroom door.

"I've been thinking about everything that's happened since I left Portland, and it's all related. Even my accident when I was hiking has to be tied in."

"I thought that was just an unfortunate fall. You fell while hiking or something."

She appreciated the concern on his face, but she shook her head and said, "I remember something." She watched as his face transformed into what she called his hulk expression. It didn't come out often, but when it did, she had always been worried about the explosive anger that followed.

"What. Are. You. Talking. About?"

Each word he spoke was punctuated with a force she had forgotten. With any luck, it wouldn't bring Clint out of the bedroom.

"I remember two men. They had been chasing me from my campsite and when I fell and was lying at the bottom of the ravine, they looked down at me, and one guy said to the other to not worry, I'd die before anyone found me."

His face morphed from anger to concern. "Paulina, that's awful. You must have been terrified."

That was a distinct memory. Even now she was still processing the heart-pounding memory of lying helpless, grateful they hadn't tried to get down the vertical hill face and finish her off.

His eyes locked on hers. "You never said who found you."

The intensity of his stare stopped her from speaking for a moment. When she found her voice, she said, "I was lucky. A group of hikers discovered me and they called for help. Once the rescue team arrived, they took me to the hospital."

He moved to kneel in front of her, taking her chilled hands in his. "Why didn't you say before that you had been under strain, all this time withholding that scary detail from your story?"

"I didn't remember it until recently. But it doesn't make any difference. I don't have any idea who they were."

"Do you think you'd recognize either of them if you saw them again?"

Thinking back to their faces, they were fuzzy, like a picture not quite in focus. "No, I don't think so." She blinked hard so she wouldn't have to remember the men but instead remain intent on the immediate issue. "We need to talk about what happened before our divorce. And you have to be honest with me."

Matthew rocked back on his heels and got up to sit back on the sofa. He stretched his arm across the low back, and for a man who had taken money that wasn't his, he was pretty casual about the whole thing.

He lifted his hands, palms up. "There's not much to tell. Other than some people think you have money that belongs to them. Sad for you, but they believed me."

"Who. Who are these people?" She heard the tone in her voice get more forceful and Matthew's eyes widened, which meant he noticed too.

"Loan sharks."

Now they were getting somewhere. "How much did you owe them?"

"Six years ago, it was seventy-five k, but now with interest compounding it's a bit more."

"I know, maybe even a million now." Disgust wasn't even a strong enough word for how she felt. "Back then, that amount was a lot, but not unreasonable. Why didn't you just pay it? Or at least work something out?" Her cheeks burned, which was not a good sign as her temper was rising each time he said something stupid. "You'd buy a car for that kind of money."

He shrugged. "At the time, I didn't think it was a big deal. But you're right, I should have."

"Instead, you packed me off for a quick divorce and I changed my name, to give me what, anonymity?"

He slammed his fist against the seat cushion. "Protection, Paulina. I was trying to protect you!"

She wasn't afraid of his temper—not anymore. She continued. "If you were trying to protect me, why on earth did you tell them I took the money?"

"I never dreamed they'd come after you." He clasped and unclasped his hands together, anguish on his face. "You have to believe me. I would never have deliberately put you in danger. You were my wife."

She could hear the pleading sound in his voice, and she relented a little. Although their marriage had been far from perfect, she was sure he'd never deliberately want her harmed. "We need to talk to them. You've stalled long enough. Do you know how to reach them?"

"No. I haven't done business with them in a long time. Trying to cut my losses and move on. If you get my meaning."

"Now you've decided to borrow money the legal way. Nice." She looked away, disgusted they were having this conversation, as if she was bargaining for her life.

"Polly, that's not fair."

Her head snapped in his direction. "You don't have the right to call me Polly. You've never met this woman. She was born that day at the bottom of the ravine when I was left for dead."

"That was not my fault. I didn't know where you were and if I had, I would have tried to do something to stop anyone from hurting you."

She softened as she saw the pain well up in his eyes. "Can you just respect the boundaries of my life? I'm trying to keep the old and new separate."

He gave her a long, appraising look. "I can tell you're different. It's as if you belong in the Podunk town, working in the dirt and driving around in an old pickup truck, wearing jeans, tee shirts, and work boots." He looked her up and down. "It's a far cry from the silk and Italian leather you used to wear."

She gave him a small smile. Matthew would never understand why she was happy here or that she found love, the real thing this time, with Clint. "Does it bother you? That I've finally come into my own?"

"No. I thought it might when I decided to come out here to see what I could do to help things along."

"I don't think you said, how did you find me?"

He leaned forward and rested his arms on his thighs. Lowering his voice, he said, "I hired a private detective. It took a while, but eventually this was his best lead. I had to call and see if you were okay and then, after I had found you, I had to come here." His voice cracked. "To finish this once and for all."

"I want it over with as well. But where do we go from here? If we need to reach out and get the money back to them, how do we find them?" She knew she sounded like a broken record, but it was all she could say.

"We don't. They'll find us, well, you really."

Her stomach flipped when he said that. The reality of people coming after her, maybe even already in town, was hard to comprehend. "If that's the case, then how can we be prepared? Are you going to take out a mortgage on the house or plan on signing it over to them?"

"I'll have the money when the time comes. For now, you keep your eyes open and watch your back. Don't trust anyone you don't know. Even some of those cowboys on that ranch you work at might not be who they seem."

Polly snapped her mouth shut after it dropped open when Matthew suggested any of the ranch hands might be behind this craziness. She knew for a fact that Linc and Clint vetted everyone who was hired, and if there had been anyone new in the last month or so, Clint would have made sure she knew about him when this all bubbled to the surface.

She thrust her chin a bit higher and made sure to project confidence to wipe that smug smile off his face. "Not to sound naïve, but I highly doubt anyone who was hired to scare me would be adept at working as a ranch hand. Contrary to what you might think, it takes skill and knowledge of this way of life to pull off getting hired at Grace Star Ranch."

"Don't be pigheaded, Paulina. You and I both know you aren't the best judge of character."

She looked him square in the eye. That comment was too much and she couldn't hold back this time. "That's rich. I married you, didn't I?"

He rose to his feet. "Mark my words, the person who's after you is right under your nose and you don't even know it." He walked to the front door and paused with his hand on the doorknob. He turned and the look on his face was almost sorrowful. "I'm sorry this is happening to you. It will be over soon."

She forced a smile and nodded. "I have good friends who will step in if necessary, but you should take your own advice. You could get caught up in the fallout, too."

"Your cowboy won't be able to protect you. But I promise, I'll find the money to pay it back, so as soon as they make contact, reach out. I'll make this right."

She wasn't sure if he expected her to express her thanks or be mad that she was in this position in the first place. "I know you will. Matthew, in some small way, it helps that you're ready to make amends and help me move on to the next phase of my life."

"It will be a fresh start."

The door closed softly behind him, and she waited until she heard his car drive away before she said, "Clint. He's gone."

Her bedroom door opened, and he stood in the doorway. His face was filled with anger. "Polly, I've got a bad feeling. Things are about to get worse and soon."

She held out her hand, and he took it as he sat next to her. "We'll get through this, and in a few weeks, we can plan another camping trip. This time maybe we'll add a hike too."

"And we'll never have to see Matthew again."

She ran her finger down his jawline. "He'll be out of our lives forever."

---

24

*T*he next day, Clint went in search of Linc. Something the ex had said last night gnawed at him. Was it possible there was someone working on the ranch who could be a threat to Polly?

When he got to the dining hall, he crossed the open space and made his way down the hallway where all the business offices were except for Annie's. She maintained her office at the main house. He rapped on the doorframe to Linc's office.

"Got a minute?"

Linc looked up from the stack of papers in front of him. If he noticed the worried look in Clint's eyes, he didn't mention it. "Have a seat."

Clint took off his hat and held it in his hands. "Thanks. I won't take up much of your time. I know you have a lot to do."

"Take all the time you need." Linc picked up his coffee mug and took a sip.

"Polly and I have been trying to figure out who could have sent her that message and shot me. Last night her ex stopped over. She was hoping to discover when someone might come around looking for the money the ex owes. He said something that's been bothering me." Clint felt like a jerk for questioning Linc on his hiring, but Polly's life wasn't anything he was willing to gamble on, and if anyone didn't like pointed questions, well, too bad.

"Go on, Clint. I can tell something's eatin' at you. Spit it out."

"How long ago did you hire the last ranch hand and did you check them out?" Now that the question was out there, it didn't sound as bad as it had floating around in his head.

Linc tapped his computer keyboard. "I'll check employment records."

After what seemed like an eternity, Linc looked up from the screen. "It was eight months ago. We hired Tate Dunn as a wrangler. He's had extensive knowledge of horses and as Annie's breeding program picks up, the plan is to give him more responsibility with it."

"His references were solid?" Clint liked Tate and couldn't picture him hurting a creature on four or two legs.

"Yes. You know we'd never hire anyone for the ranch who didn't check out, and think of how Annie loves her horses. She checked him out all the way back to middle school and when he interviewed, he said she could dig to her heart's content. He wanted to work here. So I don't think he'd be hanging around this long and suddenly change his spots."

That was a dead end. "Polly's ex insinuated that someone working on the ranch could be a potential problem."

Linc eased back in his chair. "We've got eyes on her all

the time. Ever since that incident with the mountain lion, all the hands have been keeping their eyes peeled for anything. You know Quinn keeps an eye on her, as does Jed. If you're not around, trust in your friends."

He stood and dipped his head. "Thanks, Linc. Sorry to bother you."

"Never a problem. But just how bad do you think this all is?"

"If this were a suspense book or movie, I'd say bad. But this is real life. Even though I got shot standing on her porch, I still think it was someone gunning for the ex. Not her."

"Do you trust her ex-husband?"

That sucked the wind from his lungs. The way Linc asked the question, he already knew the answer.

"Would you?"

"Not in this lifetime." Linc got up and followed him out of the office. "Do you think he'll be poking around here again?"

"It's possible. He said he'll let Polly know if anything comes up, like if the loan sharks hit town."

"Keep the lines of communication open with me and try not to worry. Polly is safe at the ranch and I'm sure if she's not here, the two of you are at her place."

"You got that right."

Linc clapped a hand on his shoulder. "I'll check in with the construction team again, too. She's got friends. This time Polly isn't facing the unknown alone."

Clint waited until after most of the hands had come in and out for lunch before seeking out Quinn. He had already talked to Jed. Not surprising when he walked into the kitchen, there was his girl, eating a bowl of soup and sopping up the fragrant broth was a thick slice of fresh bread.

"Hey you." He kissed her cheek. "How do you rate with this for lunch?"

Polly laughed. "Quinn asked if I'd test a new recipe he wanted to try, and it's a keeper." She gave Quinn a thumbs-up and a quirky wink.

"Got any more, Quinn?" His stomach made some loud grumbles; it had been a while since he'd eaten.

"Help yourself. It's on the stove." Quinn went into the walk-in refrigerator, leaving them alone.

Clint pointed to her bowl. "Another ladleful?"

She thought for half a beat and then handed him her empty bowl. "Yes, please."

He was quiet while he got the soup and returned to the table. While he spooned up bites of the tasty meal, he thought about what he wanted to say to her, without scaring her. But if the boot were on the other foot, he'd want her to shoot straight. Setting his spoon aside, he looked her in the eye. He noticed she was waiting for him to speak.

"I checked in with Linc a while ago and asked when the last hand came on board. It was Tate, you know, the horse wrangler."

She nodded and waited for him to continue. It was easy to see the question lingering in her big, round eyes.

"Your ex was off base insinuating that someone here could be the problem."

"What about the construction workers? That's how Matthew was able to track me down."

"Linc will check again, but I'm guessin' Matthew getting hired was a fluke. He must have talked a good game to get Jesse to bring him on. He likes to hire experienced people for jobs like this and takes newbies on for smaller projects."

"Makes sense." Polly got up from her chair and eased herself between the table and Clint's chest. "Can I make a suggestion?" She placed her lips on his forehead and worked her way down one side of his face and back up the other while he wondered where she was going. It was the middle of the workday and anything she started would have to wait until later.

She hovered over his lips. "Can we not spend every conversation talking about my ex-husband and get back to our dating life? I've missed that since he showed up."

There was nothing he wouldn't give for their sole focus to be on their romance. And since he'd do anything she wanted, he slipped his arms around her waist, clasping them together on the small of her back.

"How about we get dressed up tonight, all fancy like, and have dinner at the River Run Inn? It's quiet, very romantic, and has excellent desserts to go. Then we'll come back here and sit on my front porch, watching the stars. You can't get more romance packed into a night like that."

He'd do anything to keep the smile in her eyes that flickered there.

"What time do you want to pick me up?"

That would mean she was alone at her place. But he didn't want to put her in a bubble since she'd hate that and eventually him. "Six? I'll call Becky Easton and let her know."

"Great." She went to slip off his lap, and he held her in place.

"But can you do your boyfriend a favor?"

She gave him a generous grin. "That depends."

"Will you let me know when you are getting ready to leave and text when you get home? I know I sound like some overprotective jerk, but contrary to what your ex says, I believe the person who shot me is still out there and it makes me uneasy. I know you can take care of yourself, but you're not able to keep an eye on everything while you're driving. And if anything looks out of place when you get home, don't go inside, but call me first and I'll come to town."

She got to her feet and popped her hands on her hips. "Clint, you're right about sounding overprotective. I appreciate it, but I will not allow some random person to stop me from living my life. I'm going to go home and put on something pretty for our date and I swear, if you're late, well, groveling for forgiveness might be in order." She bent down and pecked at his lips. "Now I'm going to sit down and finish my lunch before going back to work, and you're going to do the same." She straightened and did as she said. "You should have wrangled a piece of bread from Quinn. It's delicious."

"Have you ever tasted a slice of bread that you didn't think was amazing?"

She grinned at the teasing tone in his voice. Closing her eyes for dramatic effect, she said, "Hm, I don't believe so. Even stale bread can be turned into stuffing or bread pudding, so that's a double win."

He couldn't help but chuckle. Clint loved how she looked at the world like everything had possibilities, and for the first time in a long time, he knew that was true.

~

*C*lint picked Polly up at six on the dot and the moment he saw her, his mouth went dry. She twirled in the doorway when she opened it, the skirt of her dress showing a glimpse of thigh. She had pulled her hair up into a bun so her neckline was exposed, begging to be kissed.

"What do you think? Good enough for a dinner date with my handsome cowboy?"

He was glad he opted for dress slacks, a button-up shirt, and a sport coat. He needed to be the frame of her perfect picture.

She frowned. "What? You don't like it?"

Stammering, he said, "No. That's not it. I'm… I'm speechless. Every time I see you, I swear you get more beautiful."

A flush slipped over her cheeks as her lips tipped up. That smile was all he ever needed to see. "I'll get my handbag."

"Did you throw some warmer clothes in another bag for stargazing?" She picked up a small backpack off the floor and handed it to him.

"I did."

He took the keys and locked up, and then before she could walk down the steps, he pulled her into his arms. "You look beautiful tonight, Polly. I can't wait to walk into the restaurant holding your hand."

She seemed to mold to his body. "I need to remind myself that you might not be quick with compliments, but they always come from your heart."

"Jeans and flannel or silk and heels. You're always the most stunning woman in the room."

"I dare say we need to get your eyes checked, but you do say the sweetest things."

He knew she was poking fun at him, but he didn't care. He only had eyes for her. *Pop! Pop!* He twirled her behind him and in one smooth motion, he withdrew a gun from under his jacket. His gaze swept the street from right to left, but he didn't see anyone.

She placed a hand on his left forearm. "I think that was a truck down the street backfiring."

He didn't look away from where he thought he had heard the shot. Even with the pressure of her hand on his arm, reminding him she was okay, he remained vigilant. After a long, silent minute, he relaxed his stance and put the handgun back in its holster.

Placing a hand on his cheek softly, she said, "You really are ready to protect me."

He pulled her close to his side, never looking away from the street. He inhaled her sweet honeysuckle perfume. "Until my last breath."

25

_P_olly woke the next morning to the smell of fresh-brewed coffee. She stretched her arms overhead, cozy in Clint's bed. He had insisted on sleeping in the recliner chair. One of these days, she was going to show him she was ready to take the next step in their relationship. But somehow, with Matthew and the mess hovering over her like a dark cloud, she wasn't ready. For her, it meant she was committing herself to him wholeheartedly. Intimacy was not something she had ever taken lightly.

She pulled on his thick velour bathrobe and padded barefoot into the living room. She leaned against the doorjamb, watching him. The throw blanket barely covered his sock-clad feet, and the weak rays of the sun highlighted his high cheekbones. She sighed. He was so handsome.

"Are you going to keep looking at me or do you want to come over and give me a proper good morning kiss?" His voice was soft and sleepy. He yawned.

How did he know she was standing there? His eyes weren't even open yet.

"You made coffee?" Her gaze drifted to the small kitchen area where a coffee maker and bread were sitting on the small counter.

"Before I went to sleep. I'm less grumpy if I don't have to wait." He opened one eye and gave her a sexy come-hither smile, which in turn caused her knees to knock just a bit. "How about I get us a mug, and then we can sit on the front porch and watch the day start?"

He dropped the footrest on the recliner with a *thunk*. "Sounds good. I'm just going to get a shirt since someone is wearing my robe."

Nonplussed, she grinned. "It's cozy, too."

Coffee poured and sitting on the front porch, Clint came out the door and took a seat next to her on the glider. "I'm glad Annie suggested I hang this glider up."

She gave in to the gentle swinging motion and tugged her feet under the hem of the robe.

"Thanks for last night." He took the mug and sipped. "Did you enjoy yourself?"

"I did." She leaned in and pecked his cheek.

"What was that for?" He put his arm around the back of the seat.

"Never rushing me. Not every man would be so patient."

"A man who pushes a woman too fast or hard isn't a real man in my book. I'm happy to be with you."

Snuggled into the crook of his arm and shoulder, she sighed as she looked out to the mountains in the distance. "I can't believe it's already August. Soon there will be snow."

"It can snow anytime in the higher elevations."

"Will it be too late to get in a hiking trip this year?" She wasn't looking forward to challenging her last fear from the accident, but it needed to be done if she wanted to put the past where it belonged.

"We'll keep to the lower elevations, and if the weather looks dicey when we make plans, we can change them." He gave her a long and steady look. Clint must have noticed she was chewing on the corner of her lip. "We can just camp and skip the hiking part."

She thought about how she wanted to respond. Was it easier to blow it off or fess up? "I need to go hiking. It's important to face that fear."

He picked up her hand and kissed the tender spot under her wrist. "Then we'll go."

Everything with Clint was so easy. Most times, he seemed to read her mind, knowing what she needed or wanted without ever having to say a word. It was as if they were on the same wavelength. It was something she had never had with Matthew.

Her cell phone chirped from inside. "The real world is intruding." She went to see who was calling. It could only be one of three people: her sister, Annie, or Matthew.

"Hello, this is an unexpected surprise."

After Matthew said hello, he continued. "I hope a good one."

She wasn't about to say one way or the other. No sense in ticking him off this early in the day. "What's up?" She knew he hated that expression, which is one of the reasons she used it.

"I was hoping you could meet me for lunch at the diner in town. I hear the food is good, and I'd really like to spend a little time with you. Alone."

"We had time a couple of days ago." She chewed on her fingernail, reverting to old habits where Matthew was concerned.

"Please, just give me one lunch since I know in my bones this mess will soon be over and I'll be going back to Portland. We won't see each other again."

Thinking about all the things she had wanted to get done today, she heard herself agree to meet at eleven thirty. "I'd like to avoid the lunch crowd and get back to work at a reasonable hour."

"Sounds like a date."

Polly didn't like how that sounded. "It's not a date, just two former spouses getting together for their almost last meal."

"See you later and say hi to your cowboy for me, too. I hope you had a good time last night."

A finger of fear slid down her spine. Had he been watching her? "How did you know we had a date last night?"

"Did you forget I'm staying at the inn? When I was walking through to my room, I saw the two of you making googly eyes at each other." He laughed. "Don't worry, Paulina. I wasn't jealous. In fact, I'm happy that you've found someone who's made you happy these last months. Everyone deserves to live their life with happiness."

Now that annoyed her. Not the part about her deserving to be happy, but the sanctimonious nonsense about him being happy for her. He wouldn't even be here if it wasn't about the money.

"See you later." She didn't want him to spew any more of his own brand of platitudes. But she wondered how Clint was going to take the news she was going to the diner for lunch.

As she walked through the door, Clint looked up. "Everything alright?"

"Fine. Matthew wants me to meet him today. And

before you ask, I agreed to an early lunch at the Filler Up."

"Oh."

Was he going to follow that up with anything? After several long, silent moments, she said, "I need to do this. He made a good point. He'll be leaving soon and you and I will go back to just being us. No looking over my shoulder, no one taking potshots at you instead of Matthew." She gave him a smile, and his started to appear.

"Maybe we'll get lucky and someone will get a shot off."

Her mouth fell open, and he held up his hand. "Just to maim him a little; after all, he's the reason this storm is swirling."

She nodded in agreement and sipped her coffee. What would it be like to just be herself, never wondering if the next shoe will drop, and actually be able to see her sister again? Maybe she'd come out to Montana for a couple of weeks next spring when all the trees and flowers started to bloom. There was no place like big sky country when the earth began to wake up. She stole a glance at Clint and smiled. Who knows, maybe there would be another reason to celebrate next year too.

26

*C*lint paced the length of the dining hall, waiting for Polly to return from lunch with Matthew. As they had agreed, she texted when she arrived and left, and that last one had him on edge.

Coming straight to the dining hall. Meet me there.

The curtness of the message made him wonder what the freaking ex had done to upset her. If it was terrible, why didn't she just ask for him to come to the diner and get her? He looked at his phone again to check the time like he had done every few seconds since he had gotten her message. She should pull up in less than five minutes.

Dust clouds swirled out from behind what looked like her truck. He ran through the room and flung open the door, taking the steps two at a time. He had her door open before it was even in park.

He could see her face was white and drawn, her lower lip pulled in while her top bit down. Whatever that man had done, he would pay.

With a strangled cry, she almost leaped into his open arms. He held her. Her breath was short and shallow. She was shaking. He held her, murmuring that she was safe. He could wait until she was ready to tell him what had gone on at the diner.

"Can we go inside?" Her voice was muffled against his shoulder.

Supporting her with an arm around her waist, he held her up as they walked, his anger growing. The door opened and Quinn was standing there, a silent centurion. Once the door was closed behind them, he left the room. He eased her down on a large leather sofa that looked out over the ranch. The view had a calming effect most of the time, and he hoped it would work again.

Within minutes, Quinn was back with tea. He knelt down. "Polly, do you want me to call Annie?"

"Linc and Jed should be here, too." She looked at Clint. "Okay?"

He nodded. "Thanks, Quinn. We'll be right here."

"Do you want to talk before the gang gets here?"

"You know how I like to face the door when I'm at the diner?"

He smiled. "You like to see who's coming and going."

Nodding, she said, "Really, I like to see what everyone is ordering, so maybe next time I'll try something different."

Her smile was weak, but at least now she wasn't shaking as hard. He continued to rub the warmth back into her ice-cold hands.

"When I was having lunch with Matthew, he said that he was sorry this had happened, but assured me he was confident it would be over soon. Which of course made me feel loads better. We were getting ready to go just after he signed the credit card slip. I looked around the diner. It was getting crowded. Sitting at the counter was a man. At first, I didn't recognize him, so I glanced away, and then I got up. That's when he looked at me. He gave me an evil smile that froze my feet to the floor and with his finger pointed at me, he mimed a push motion."

Clint's heart wanted to leap out of his chest. "Did you recognize him?"

She nodded and swallowed hard. "He was one of the men I saw when I looked up after the fall. It all clicked into place like pieces of a puzzle. And I remember the other man, too."

He wrapped his arms around her, thinking she was going to cry, but no sounds came. She must be numb from what she had experienced, and he berated himself for not going with her. He could have sat at the counter.

"Darlin', it's okay. You're safe now. But we need to call Sheriff Blackstone and see if he can get someone to sketch this guy from your description." What he didn't say was this was a direct threat against her life and there was no way she was going anyplace other than this ranch without him.

"I know. That's why I want to talk to everyone. I'm hoping I can describe him enough so people can keep a lookout." She shuddered again. "Clint, he actually looked happy when he was doing the push motion. Like he enjoyed seeing me go over the edge."

"I won't let him get to you. Try not to worry."

Clint pulled out his phone and placed a call to the sheriff, asking him to come out to the ranch. He gave a brief overview of what was going on. The sheriff had said he'd track down someone to do the illustration and be out just as soon as he could.

She hugged him tight and buried her head in his chest. She stayed there until the rest of their friends came in.

Annie took a spot on the other side of Polly. Linc, Quinn, and Jed pulled up chairs, and she went through the story a second time.

Annie took her hand. "What do you need from us?" She scanned the group, and the men nodded, their faces grim.

"Is anyone good friends with Maggie from the diner? Maybe we could find out if she knows how long this guy has been around, if she even remembers him."

Jed said, "Maggie and I are good friends. I can swing by there today and see if she remembers seeing the guy and if he's been hanging around. I'll go into town as soon as we're done here."

The pressure on Clint's chest lightened a bit. This was his family and over the last year, they had pulled Polly into their circle.

"Daphne is a designer. She might be able to draw this person. If it's okay, I'll call her to come down." Annie looked at Linc. "Once we get that done we can circulate it, post it on the bulletin board, and make sure if anyone sees this guy, to let us know right away."

Linc agreed. "I'll call up to the main house and ask her to come down." He left the room and headed to his office, probably to fill her in too before she came down.

"What about the hands taking turns at the gate and checking everyone who tries to come on the ranch?" Quinn got up from the chair and looked out toward the barns. "I know there are a ton of ways to get on the property and we can't protect the entire perimeter, but the key access might be enough of a deterrent."

"Thanks, Quinn. That's another good idea." Clint could see this was taking a toll on Polly. "You can stay at the ranch until this is over. Your ex seems to think the end is near. He must know something he's not telling. Tomorrow, let's have him come out. Since it's Saturday, there are no construction workers, so he'll be the only person who isn't supposed to be on the property. It might make it easier if someone comes skulking around."

"It is time to wrap this up. Even though Matthew is dangling from the end to this nightmare like a worm to a hungry fish, I need to take control of my life. I didn't fight back from that fall to be sitting on the hot seat, waiting for him to take care of things."

Clint sat up straighter. The shock of seeing that guy was finally wearing off, and he was relieved. Polly needed to be ready to fight like the devil to come out on top. She had it in her, but she needed to find it again. "I'll take you back to your place and you can get some clothes and plan on staying at my place."

"We have a security system at the main house. Why don't you both stay with Linc and me? There's plenty of room and Polly will be safer there than in your cabin."

Shaking her head, she thanked Annie for the offer, but she wanted to stay with Clint in his cabin. "I'm safe with him."

"I understand. If you change your mind, the door is always open." She grinned, trying to lighten the oppressive tension in the room. "Well, after you enter the security code."

The puttering sound of a golf cart outside reached Clint's ears. That had to be Daphne. Who knew the wedding planner turned resort manager would be an artist too?

The front door flew open, and Daphne entered, carrying a large pad and pencils in her hand. She rushed over, her eyes locked on Polly. Clint stood and let her sit down, since it was obvious that was her intention.

"Polly, I'm so sorry you're going through this, but I'll do my best to draw this person so that we'll know who to watch for." She looked at Quinn and back to Polly. "Do you want to do this just the two of us or would it help to have everyone here?"

She looked at each person sitting in a semicircle around her and gave them a shaky smile. "Thank you for coming and for your support. But I'm okay for now."

Everyone took the cue to head back to their jobs. Clint stayed.

"I'm sure you have something that needs your attention besides me." She pointed in the direction of his office. "Go work. I'm fine right here and I won't leave the building unless someone is with me."

Clint was torn between doing as she asked or giving in to his own fear. If he left, would something happen while he was gone? Irrational, yes, but this was the woman he loved.

"You know where I am, but when the sheriff arrives, I want to be with you during the conversation."

Now she gave him a genuine smile. "Don't worry. The sheriff makes me nervous with those dark eyes and jet-black hair. It's like just looking at a person he can tell their entire life story."

"He's a softie once you get to know him, but don't tell him I said that." Clint kissed her lips and reluctantly went down the hall.

He walked into Linc's office, where he and Annie were talking about what had happened.

Annie drew him into a hug. "I wish there was something more we could do to help. I feel like the ranch isn't secure enough to keep out riffraff."

"We'll protect her and I'm sure we'll get this guy even if we have to use the ex to help us." It was hard to keep the scowl off his face and the disgust from his voice.

"What I don't get is how could this guy who supposedly loved his wife throw her to the wolves like that? The man had to know they'd come after her." Linc didn't bother to control his anger as his fist connected with the desk. "Polly is as sweet as they come. I guess he just didn't care enough about her."

Clint realized they didn't know the full story. "He said they needed the divorce to protect her, like if she just disappeared, they'd forget about her. But now that she recognized one of the men responsible for her accident, I have to say I hope he trails the ex to learn the truth." He looked at Annie and Linc's wedding picture on the corner of his desk. That's what he wanted with Polly. "Maybe I should head into town after Daphne is finished and see if I can track this guy down. Someone has to have seen him."

Linc said, "Let Jed talk to Maggie. If anyone knows what's going on in town, it'll be her. Everyone comes through the diner. It's like a magnet. The food is good, and the price is right."

Quinn came around the corner and poked his head in the doorway. "The sheriff is here."

"Come on. Let's see what he thinks we should do next."

~

*C*lint and Polly drove back to town in his truck. First stop was her place to get clothes, and then she wanted to swing by the inn and see if Matthew was around. She wanted to show him the drawing Daphne had completed.

"I hope Matthew saw this guy, too." She stared out the window as the meadows slipped by. "I'm sure it would be too much to hope that he knows him from when he was involved with the loan shark." She turned and looked at Clint. "Right?"

All he wanted to do was hold her and tell her everything was going to be fine. But he didn't know how quickly it would happen. The sheriff took the original picture after Linc had made a bunch of copies and said he was going to check with contacts in the Portland area. With any luck, they could track him down that way and then figure out when he got to town.

When they got to Polly's, her front door was hanging off its hinges and chunks of the door were scattered on the porch. "Clint!"

He threw the truck in park and withdrew his gun. "I want you to stay here and let me check it out. Keep the doors locked and have your pistol ready."

"But out here, I'm a sitting duck. Windows on all four sides."

His heart sank. That was an accurate statement, and he wished he thought to bring Quinn with them. He would have been another set of eyes.

"Stay behind me and if anyone shoots, drop low and take cover." He gave her a quick and hard kiss. "I love you, Polly." He had to say those words. The adrenaline kicked in and who knew what they were going to discover when they got inside the house.

"Wait, I'll call the police. At least reinforcements will be on the way."

This woman kept her cool. She dialed and reported the break-in and asked for a police car right away.

They both got out and left the truck doors standing open. Polly was behind Clint. His heartbeat had slowed, and he was focused. Scanning the area for anyone who might still be around, they cautiously climbed the three steps and made their way across the porch. He poked his head in and back, then looked again before walking inside, being careful not to make much noise.

The living room looked empty, but they had ripped apart the room. Books were on the floor, cushions ripped to shreds. He pointed to the kitchen. From what they could see, it was much the same in there. They crept down the short hallway and stopped short. Food boxes had been ripped open, the contents spilled on the floor. They propped the refrigerator open and even in there, food was dripping out of containers.

He glanced at Polly and her face was devoid of all expression. He touched her arm and pointed back into the living room, and then they made their way into the bedroom. This room was the worst so far. Clothes were everywhere. The mattress had been cut and was now destroyed. They had turned every dresser drawer upside down and the closet was empty, with all its contents on the floor too.

From deep inside her, a small moan escaped Polly. "Clint, this is such a mess."

He heard the unmistakable catch in her voice, and he held open his arm so she could step into it.

"*Police!*" Thundering footsteps came into the house. "*Freeze!*"

When the sheriff saw that it was Clint and Polly, he lowered his revolver and surveyed the destruction. "Any idea who did this?"

"No, unless it was the person who shot me." Clint held Polly a little tighter. "I guess you could surmise someone was hell-bent on searching her house and my guess, they were ticked when they didn't find what they were looking for."

Sheriff Blackstone looked at them. "Sorry to say, still no leads on the shooter."

She looked up, her eyes filled with fear. "They're never going to stop. I have to talk to Matthew and get the exact dollar amount so I can pay them off." She looked around her bedroom. "What if I had been home? Would they have killed me?"

That question struck Clint to the core. Maybe that was their intent. They had tried once and failed.

27

*P*olly pulled weeds and glanced at her watch. Matthew was coming out to the ranch after lunch and one way or another, she was going to get the truth out of him if it was the last thing she did. There had to be a way to stop these lunatics from coming after her and it was time Matthew stood up and was a man instead of tossing his former wife to the wolves. She sat back on her heels and thought of Clint and the caliber of man he was by comparison. As sad as it was, there was no comparison.

A small shadow fell over her from behind and she knew it was most likely Annie. To her surprise, Mary was walking in her direction with slow but sure steps. How this woman who was north of seventy worked as hard as anyone and made it look easy, she didn't know. She hoped she was as spry as Mary was later in life.

"Hi, Mary. This is an unexpected treat." Polly stood and brushed her dirt-covered hands on her jeans.

"Annie has been keeping me abreast of what's been goin' on with you, and I hope you don't mind."

Of course, Annie told both Mary and Daphne everything. They needed to be on guard, too. She hugged the thin older woman, who had become more like a grandmother to her instead of a friend. "I'm glad Annie has kept you in the loop. It's been really tough these last couple of weeks."

"Sweet girl, I wanted you to know I'm always ready with a cup of tea or coffee and a friendly ear if you ever need to talk."

The older woman's smile was warm and came from her heart. "Thank you, Mary. That means a great deal to me. With any luck, this will be behind us soon and we can get back to the business at hand." She swept her arm over the field. "The harvest and preserving."

Mary crossed her arms over her body and grinned. "Quinn has his work cut out for him."

Looping her arm through Mary's, she said, "Come with me. I want to show you a new variety of winter squash I grew. I've got plenty to put in the root cellar if you want to take one up to the main house for tonight."

With a twinkle in her eye, Mary squeezed Polly's arm. "That would be a nice treat. A hearty squash soup might be in order too. And I will make sure to put a cup aside for your lunch tomorrow."

Walking through the garden and showing Mary everything, talking about next year's plan put a sense of balance and normalcy back into her day, and this was just what she needed before she talked with Matthew.

As they approached the gate to the house, Polly's steps slowed. "Mary, how do you do it?"

"I'm not sure what you mean. Talk about gardening almost as much as you do?"

"How can you take all the jangled nerves inside of me and smooth them out with a simple conversation?"

She beamed. "Ah, that's something Pippa often said. Annie's grandmother was my best friend, and she was a worrier as a young woman. After Annie's parents died in the plane crash, it got worse. Her grandfather loved Pippa, but he never got the hang of a calming conversation. I guess after all those years of talking with Pippa, it just became second nature to me."

Throwing her arms around Mary, she hugged her tight. "Pippa was very lucky to have a good friend in you."

Patting her cheek, Mary gestured to the house. "There are two women inside who would be the same for you. It's okay to open up and let more people into your life. I can promise they'll never hurt or betray you. True blue women. And if you don't believe me, ask Daphne sometime how she came to live at the ranch. I'd like to think a little touch of me is in Annie."

Now there was something to think about, opening up and letting more people than just Clint in her life. Maybe it was time to become an active part of the community. Other than her sister, she had never really been good at having female friends. They seemed to always be looking to come out on top when she was living in Portland.

"Give it some thought." Mary took the squash from Polly and walked through the gate toward the back door. Over her shoulder, she called, "Stop in the kitchen around four. Clint's going to be running a bit late and we'll have coffee and I made blondies." She lifted her hand in Polly's direction before closing the door behind her.

Before going back to work, she made a detour to the dining hall where she had stored her lunch in the refrigerator. Mary was right about many things. She needed more friends. She was lucky to have Quinn and Jed whom she had become close with. They were two good men who liked her and not because she was dating Clint. With her steps lighter, she hurried down the path. But a shiver raced down her spine. She did a slow three sixty but there was no one around as far as she could see. That would be all she needed, her unfriendly mountain lion to come around again. Still feeling hinky, she touched the butt of her handgun under her shirt. If anyone had told her a year ago she'd be walking in a garden with a gun, she would have scoffed at them. She wanted to jog to the kitchen, but if there was a big cat roaming, that would just encourage it to chase her. The last thing she needed was more danger.

Polly texted Matthew about two o'clock and said she was in the greenhouse. Several minutes later, he said he'd meet her there. Her stomach tightened at the thought of the direct conversation she needed to have with him, but it was long overdue. He was going to stop dancing around the subject and tell her everything. She stamped her foot for an extra kick of adrenaline to her system. While she was doing the inventory, her phone pinged. She looked at the message from her sister and sent a quick text back. *Call you tonight.* She got a smiley face emoji back and put her phone on the workbench.

The sound of a door slamming caught her attention, and she looked up to see Matthew striding toward her. His smile was jovial, almost a little too carefree. Didn't he care about what was happening to her?

"Paulina, don't you look in your element?"

He tucked a strand of her hair back behind her ear. The hair on her arms rose to attention, and she rubbed her hand over her shirtsleeve. Moving to the other side of the bench, she kept lining up pots, and she forced a smile.

"You know I've always loved gardening and now I can do it on a large scale."

"What would these cowboys do without your skill of making food grow from little seeds?" He picked things up and set them down, not really looking at them but all the while keeping his eyes on her. "So, I'm here. What was so important? You wanted to talk today."

"Well," she said, letting the word slide out slowly, "during lunch yesterday, I saw a man who I think shoved me into the ravine."

The smile evaporated from his face, and she breathed a sigh of relief. The news seemed to upset him just as much as it did her.

"Did he speak to you?"

The tone of his voice made her stomach flip. "No, but he gave me a knowing smile and then a pushing motion and he smirked."

"Why didn't you tell me on the spot? I would have done something." He tipped his head. "Wait, do you mean the guy with the long nose, a few days' growth of whiskers, and bald?"

"Yes, that's the guy. You saw him." At least he could provide some details to the police. "Any idea where he is staying? The police are looking for him."

"I think he's left town and won't be smirking at you again."

"Why? What makes you say that?"

Matthew stepped around the side of the bench and was coming in her direction. His lips had formed a thin, unforgiving line. He shrugged. "Let's just say we had a chat, and I pointed him in a different direction."

"Matthew, what exactly are you talking about?" She

snapped her head up and glared at him. "Does that mean you saw him make that gesture to me?"

He lifted one shoulder and shrugged. "Paulina, I have to admit. I do—or did—know him and his friend. But I can promise you neither of them will ever hurt you again."

She took a step back, running her hand down the bench to help her stay connected to reality since this conversation was becoming surreal. "Matthew, you're scaring me."

"I really wanted this to be easy for you, but a little fear will just be a part of our new situation."

"What are you talking about? We have to get the money to the loan sharks, and then we'll both be in the clear."

He snorted and was shaking his head, all the while never breaking eye contact. "For a smart woman, you really haven't figured all this out yet, have you?"

She enunciated each word carefully to keep her voice from shaking. "Figured out that you know some pretty crappy people? That has become clear."

"There was never a loan shark, and I owed no one money, but you owe me some money and it's almost time for me to collect."

She stumbled back and tripped over a bag of peat moss. "I don't have any money, you know that. I left everything behind when I moved to Nevada, and when I went on the run, I took even less." Her mind raced. What could he be talking about?

Matthew reached out and grabbed her arm with enough force to keep her from getting away, but not enough to really hurt her. "Two words. Life insurance."

"What are you talking about?" With her shirt buttoned

she couldn't reach her gun, but on the other hand, he couldn't see it either.

"There is a multimillion-dollar life insurance policy on my beloved wife that I just happened to forget about canceling when we got divorced. Magically, I'll discover it when I'm gathering papers for your funeral." He picked up her hand and kissed the back of it. "Just in case I forget to tell you later, I want to thank you for setting me up financially for the rest of my life."

It hit home. He planned on killing her to collect the money.

He gestured to the door. "Come on now, it's time we go for a brief ride around the ranch. I have just the spot for our last conversation before you meet your maker."

A cold sweat broke out over her skin. She glanced toward the barn.

"Don't worry about your cowboy. He's currently being watched and if he decides to be a hero or come back early, he'll be waiting for you on the other side."

28

*C*lint took the path at a jog on his way to the greenhouse. He couldn't wait to see Polly and plan what they were making for dinner. When he got there, the door was ajar. He walked in and called out for her. The silence engulfed him. He walked up and down each row of benches and at the end, he saw her cell phone. She never went anywhere without it.

"Polly?" His voice kicked up, and he yelled again. "Polly!"

He took her phone and ran at full speed to the dining hall. Going in the back door, he skidded to a stop. "Quinn, have you seen Polly?"

"Not since lunch. She was here for about a half hour, said the ex was coming by around two, and she was going to the main house for coffee."

That was it. She had to be with Annie. He thanked him and took off at a dead run. His heart was in this throat and he flung open the back door. Mary was the only person in the kitchen. Taking gulps of air, he said, "Where's Polly?"

Confusion flashed across Mary's face. "I'm not sure.

She was coming up for coffee around four and never showed up. I assumed you had gotten done early and the two of you were together."

He shook his head. "I just got back. She's not in the greenhouse and her phone and truck are both there. I have to find her." Panic squeezed his throat. He knew in his gut something bad had happened. He turned to the door. "Where's Linc?"

"Hold on. He's with Annie in the office." Mary left the kitchen, and he heard her calling for his friends.

The three of them were back within moments, but it seemed like hours.

Linc asked, "What's happened?"

"It's Polly. I don't know where she is, and no one has seen her since lunch." He paced around the room. "I have to find her."

Annie had left the room unnoticed but was handing Linc a walkie. "Start calling the hands, see if anyone has seen her."

Linc sent out a general call for anyone knowing where Polly's location was. Over the next ten minutes, Linc was checking off each report. No one had seen her, and oddly, Jed hadn't checked in either.

"Could she and Jed have gone off someplace?" Annie asked as she placed a comforting hand on his arm.

"Why would they? They're both focused on their jobs during the day. Unless they were working in the garden, Jed would take care of the horses." The words died on his lips and he turned and headed out to the horse barn with Linc and Annie on his heels.

Annie had called out for Mary to contact the sheriff and report a missing person.

Linc pulled open the sliding barn door. Jed's grooming

tools were scattered on the floor, and the place was in a general state of someone working who hadn't completed the job. "Jed?"

Annie ran the length of the barn, checking each stall. Clint hoped he was working and just didn't hear them and not crumpled in a ball from being kicked in the head by a horse.

Annie called from the end. "He's not here."

Linc called his cell, and it went to voicemail. He left him a message to call in, saying it was urgent. He put his phone back in his shirt.

The walkie squawked. "Quinn here."

"Yes, Quinn."

"The hands are coming in, asking questions about Polly."

"Ask them if anyone has seen Jed. We're on our way up. And tell everyone to stay put."

With each passing minute, Clint knew Polly was in grave danger, and he did not know how to help her. Yet.

In the dining hall, most of the ranch hands were sitting at tables, food in front of them, but not eating. Clint, Linc, and Annie burst through the door and idle talk stopped as all eyes turned to them.

Clint wasn't about to wait for Linc or Annie. "Listen up, everyone. Polly's phone and truck are at the greenhouse, but no one has seen her since noon when she grabbed her lunch from the refrigerator. She had a meeting with her ex at two. But she was threatened again when she was at the diner. So I have to know, who saw what?"

At first, everyone remained silent. Then Blake Marshall said, "Jed was gonna check on her midafternoon. You should ask him."

"Jed is missing too," Clint stated. The band tightened around his chest.

Blake said, "It's not like Jed would run off with Polly, you know."

"That thought never crossed my mind, but does anyone know anything at all? Did you see or hear anything?"

Tate, one of the horse wranglers, said, "I heard a single shot around three but didn't think much about it. Figured someone was shooting a snake or something."

Feeling the color drain from his face, Clint whirled around and looked at Linc and Annie. "Do you think she was?" He couldn't even bring himself to say the word killed.

Annie stepped forward and grabbed his arm. "No, never happened. We don't know if it was a shot or not. You know how sound travels out here. For now, we are going to assume that Polly and Jed are fine and maybe even together." She said, "Quinn, can you brew coffee? Linc, get maps of the ranch and town. We'll set up search parties, and when the sheriff arrives, we'll be ahead of the game." She looked around the room at the men looking back at her. Clint could see the determination on their faces. They'd give their all to bring Polly and Jed home. And so would he.

❧

The next morning, Clint was running on fumes as he dragged himself into the dining hall to get coffee and breakfast. He didn't want to take the time, but if he was going to be any good to Polly at all, he needed to be strong. Other than basic chores, every ranch hand was gearing up for another day of searching. Was it foolhardy to think they hadn't gotten off the ranch? Before he made it inside, his cell rang.

"News?" he demanded.

It was Linc. "We found a car that is registered to Matthew Parker. Doors open with no one inside."

"Where?" He threw open the double doors, ready to relay information to the men inside.

"Do you remember the old entrance to Annie's parents' spread east of the main entrance to Grace Star?"

"Yeah. Haven't been out there in years."

"Annie found the car in the tree line about two hundred yards in from the road."

A flicker of hope that Polly was going to be found alive flared in his chest. "Wait, the ex's car? It was empty?"

"Yes. Clint, we found dried blood on the back seat."

His blood ran cold. If he hurt Polly, there was nothing that was going to stop him from tearing the ex limb from limb. "I'll have the hands meet us there and we'll search. Ask Annie if she can think of any good places to hole up." He didn't want to say what was really on his mind—if there was a good place to dump a body. He couldn't say that out loud. "I'll be there as fast as I can."

"I've called the sheriff and requested air support out here, too." Linc was doing all he could to move things along.

"I'm on my way." He strode inside. About ten ranch hands were in various stages of eating. They had been searching all night and deserved a break, but they needed feet on the ground.

"Listen up." All the hands gave him their undivided attention. "Annie discovered a car inside the old gates of her parents' place just east of here. There's a strong possibility it was the car Polly was in when she left the ranch. We need to get search parties scouring the area. Get something to eat and meet me there as soon as you can."

Quinn was standing in the swinging doorway. "Give me a minute and I'll come with you."

Clint strode across the room. "I need you here feeding everyone. Someone needs to be around if Polly or Jed come back. We need eyes and ears here, too."

He got where Quinn was coming from. If someone he considered a friend was missing, he would want to be searching, but it made sense and he needed someone at the ranch he trusted.

Quinn met his gaze. "Go. But have someone keep me in the loop and if either of them shows up, I'll call."

There were no words Clint could have said at that moment. Quinn nodded in the direction of the door. "Go."

He didn't have to be told twice. He ran back the way he had come and jumped in his pickup. He briefly wondered if they might need men on horses or UTVs. If they did, they'd work it out.

It seemed to take years off his life as he raced to the homestead. When he arrived, he saw Linc's pickup beside the old house. Someone had taken good care of it, but it looked as if no one had been in it for quite some time. The short-lived hope that she was being held inside died when he saw Linc shake his head.

"A bunch of men will be over soon." Clint looked around. "Where do we start?"

Annie said, "There are a few caves but in opposite directions from each other. As a kid I used to play in one more than the others since it was bigger. Less chance of bats and other creepy things."

"Which way? I'll go there first." Clint looked between Annie and Linc. "What are we waiting for?"

"You need to see this." Linc walked down an overgrown path. "Look."

His heartbeat slowed as he saw the trail of blood. It was going off to the right. "Do you think this is an animal?" But he knew it was human. There weren't signs of a scuffle, but something large had been dragged. Was it Polly or Jed?

"Afraid not." Linc nodded back to the truck. "Get your shotgun and we'll get going."

Clint ran back to the truck and withdrew his phone as it rang. "Quinn?"

"Just letting you know twenty guys are headed your way."

"Thanks." He put his phone on vibrate and jammed it back into his shirt pocket. No sense letting the entire world know he was around.

29

*I*nside the cave, the first light of day barely made a difference to how much Polly could see. Her head ached where Matthew had hit her before dragging her out of the greenhouse. A soft groan came from the mound next to her. She hoped they were alone for a minute. She needed to check on Jed.

She inched closer, despite her hands and feet being bound. In a whisper, she said, "Jed. Open your eyes."

He groaned again as he struggled against the ropes around his wrists and feet. Leaning over, she whispered in his ear to lie still. She needed to get her hands free so she could get to her gun. There was no way she was going to allow them to be sitting ducks for Matthew when he returned from wherever he had gone.

Jed rolled over and seemed to wiggle his fingers. He wanted to get her untied. She scooted along the cold cave floor until his fingers grazed her hands. Holding still, she could feel him trying to untie them. The ropes were loosening. She wanted to tell him to hurry, but talking wouldn't help. He understood the urgency. After all, he'd been trying to help her when Matthew knocked him unconscious and tossed him into the trunk. When they got to the old ranch, he forced Polly to get Jed out of the back seat and help drag him to the cave. The entire time she was trying to figure out a way to shoot him, the low-life scum. But the way he had tied her hands and feet, all she could do was half drag Jed.

She blinked back the tears of regret that her friend had gotten involved. No one should have to be here with her. She planned to convince Matthew to leave Jed in the cave, that his head injury would kill him. That way, he wouldn't be facing a murder rap besides kidnapping. Not that she had any intention of letting Jed die. Her ex-husband was going down, one way or the other.

She tugged on her ropes, and they gave way. Now to fake still being secured. Jed rolled back over to his previous position. Which was perfect since this was all a head game now. It didn't require physical strength. But before she ended this, she needed answers.

It wasn't long before Matthew entered the cave, ducking his head until he got farther in. Polly should know; she smacked her head last night and saw stars for the second time in one day, and not the good kind.

How was it possible she could have smart remarks running around in her head, considering that she was facing the end of her life?

"Good morning, dear wife. I'm glad to see you're awake."

Although Polly couldn't see him clearly, he had used that phrase enough times during their marriage she could picture the benign smile on his face.

"Matthew, so what's our plan for today?"

He tipped his head as if surprised, but not at the sass in her voice. "You want to know the events leading up to the big ending? You always did read the last chapter in a book first."

"Can you blame me?"

"I guess not. Well, in a little while you and I will take a walk, after of course, I finish your friend over there. It really is too bad he's not your boyfriend. I would have enjoyed the pleasure of seeing your face as his life ebbed away, knowing that you were the reason."

Despite the overwhelming desire to scream and lunge at him, she forced herself to keep a cool head. Now was the time where she could attempt to save Jed. "I've been thinking about that. With his head injury, our location, and lack of water, he won't last long as it is, so why don't we just leave him here? That way, you won't have two murder raps hanging over your head."

"Paulina, I have quite a few. You and that cowboy are just two more. Even if I were ever to get caught, I can't serve more than one life sentence, but after I receive your life insurance money, I'm moving to a sunny beach to live out the rest of my life in quiet tranquility."

She blanched at the thought of him casually saying she and Jed would just be two more. "Did you kill that guy from the diner?" The last thing she wanted to know was if he had just killed someone, but she also needed to know.

"Don't worry about him. After he botched your last accident along with his buddy, well, they became expendable."

"You killed them?" The glint in his eye made a shiver race down her back. "How could I not know the real man you are? Did you ever love me, or was this always your plan?"

He sat down on a small rock and crossed his legs. The revolver was in plain sight, and she would not underestimate what kind of shot he was. He was the one who taught her how to handle a gun.

"Don't be upset with yourself. I only let you see what I wanted you to see." He waved the gun around. "But things could have been different if we'd had a kid. You never kill the mother of your child."

"We agreed to wait." Not that she would have wanted to have a baby with this monster. How could she keep him talking and buy extra time? By now, people had to be out looking for her and Jed. Would anyone even think about looking on the ranch? Most people who were taken ended up far away from the scene of the abduction. At least that's what she read in newspaper accounts.

"I can tell your brain is working overtime. What's going on behind those ordinary hazel eyes?"

"You didn't used to say that I was ordinary in any way. You'd say I was beautiful."

With a snort of rude laughter, he said, "And you believed me, hook, line, and sinker. Right down to where I said I was divorcing you for your safety. How could you be so stupid?"

That did it. Telling her she was stupid set off all kinds of emotions. "Well, if I had known I was married to and living with a psychopath, I would never have believed a word you said."

"Temper." He got up and walked to where she was on the ground. "You wouldn't want me to kill you right here. It will be so much more effective than what I have planned. It's important that your body is discovered. No body, no money."

He reached out his hand, almost as if he was about to caress her face when she glared at him. "I would think very carefully before you touch me."

"I wasn't going to mar your face. I'm not a monster."

She never blinked. "Debatable."

"The plastic surgeon did a wonderful job. He kept the essence of you while enhancing it." He settled back on the rock and said, "You know, that is one thing I've always admired about you—your grit. You never give in, even when it looks as if all is lost. You keep trying to find a window to crawl through. This time, there are no windows, doors, or even a mousehole that will get you out of this predicament. Is there anything else you want to talk about before we leave this cozy little cave and I show you the special spot I've chosen for you and that wannabe hero lying in a heap behind you?"

"You never answered my question."

"Oh, yes. I wondered if you'd get back to that." He looked away, and when he looked back, in the dim light, he almost looked remorseful. "When we were dating, I cared for you. This idea was faint. It was only after the first anniversary that things changed."

"If you thought things had changed, why didn't you talk to me? We could have fixed it." Her hands were completely untangled from the ropes, and now she was wondering how fast she could get to her gun and get a shot off before he shot her. Or worse, before he shot Jed.

Matthew shrugged. "It didn't matter that much once I realized I could insure you for millions very cheap. You were young and for a ten-year-term policy, the decision was easy." He snapped his fingers and got up. "And the policy expires next month."

She watched as a mask fell over his face and a hardness hovered in his eyes. With the set of his mouth, she knew her time was up. A loud crash echoed inside the cave as the ground shook. Polly feared they were going to be crushed by rocks.

He pointed to her and growled, "Stay put."

The minute he turned, she ripped open the chambray shirt and felt the butt of the revolver with her hand. She eased it out, not making a sound. The last thing she needed was for Matthew to turn around. Moving as quickly as her tied feet would allow, she got to her knees and took aim at the opening. With any luck, even in these dim conditions, she could take him down and leave enough of him to go to trial all while protecting Jed, who was rolling over, hopefully to get out of the way. He was in no shape to help her and besides, his hands and feet were still bound.

The seconds dragged. Her arms quivered from holding them straight out of her body, but she wasn't giving in.

In her ear, Jed whispered, "Steady."

She didn't dare respond. She waited. A branch crunched under what had to be Matthew's foot. A silhouette filled the cave entrance. She took aim at his right shoulder and pulled the trigger. He got a shot off before buckling to his knees.

Matthew screamed, "You shot me!"

The sounds of people rushing the entrance had Polly remaining in position. Maybe he had people helping him.

"Polly!" It was Clint's voice. He had come for her.

She wanted to sob with relief, but she kept her gun

trained on Matthew. "In here. Be careful. Matthew has a gun."

Clint rushed in first, his shotgun at the ready. When his eyes met Polly's, he called for Linc to deal with Matthew, and he rushed to her side. She sank to the floor as it began to register she was cold and the floor unforgiving. But she and Jed were going to see another sunrise.

"Help Jed first." She tried to untie the ropes on her feet when Annie reached her. She withdrew a knife.

"Let me."

Clint said, "Take care of Jed. I've got Polly."

Annie cupped her cheek and smiled. "It's good to see you."

She nodded. "It's good to be seen."

After making quick work of the rope around her ankles, Clint took off his jacket and wrapped it around her shivering body. Then he scooped her up and took her outside. She looked at Matthew in a heap outside the cave. Even though she wanted to bury her head in Clint's shoulder, she asked him to put her down.

Matthew smirked. "You've lost your touch, Paulina. Back in the day, you would have hit me in the heart."

The utter hate she felt for him was barely controlled as she said, "No. I haven't. My aim was true. Not taking your life means you'll pay for the lives you've taken. Rot in jail, Matthew."

She gave Linc a curt nod, and Annie was helping Jed out of the cave. He had dried blood on his forehead and his eyes were black and bruised, but he, too, was alive.

Without hesitation, she rushed him, throwing her arms around his neck and squeezing with all her might. "Thank you for trying to save me."

He went scarlet. "You deserve all the credit." He

looked at Clint. "They broke the mold with this one. You best be good to her or I'll, well, I won't need to do a thing. Polly's got this covered." He bent over and kissed her cheek. "Way to go, cowgirl. You're one of us, you know."

Clint slipped his arm around Jed's shoulders. "I guess we're all lucky she wound up at Grace Star Ranch." He looked deep into her eyes and his voice dropped as he said, "But me most of all."

30

*I*t had been three weeks since the kidnapping, and Polly lay wrapped securely in Clint's arms. The fire crackled in front of them, warming her toes as the dark blanket of stars appeared above them. She sighed, completely content to not move a muscle for the next week. Or however long it was before the snow flew at this elevation.

"That was a heavy sigh." His breath warmed her cool cheeks.

"This moment is so perfect. I was just thinking we can stay right here until the snow flies."

He chuckled. "Other than eating and running out of wood, it sounds like a perfect plan." He pulled a soft wool blanket over them.

"I'm sorry about everything that happened since the ex showed up." Would he notice she no longer referred to him by his name? It had never bothered her that Clint always referred to him as "the ex" as if speaking his name gave him more power in their lives.

"None of what happened was your fault. You were the victim, long before you even knew what was going on. Being set up by your ex is the most despicable thing I've ever heard of. To, over time, gaslight you into thinking someone was after you." His voice grumbled out the next statement. "He's going to spend the rest of his life thinking about how he was outmaneuvered by you. I hope someone puts a shiv in him. But behind bars is the perfect place for him to live out his life since he almost took yours."

She shivered, but this time not from the chill in the air but from his words. Clint wasn't wrong. It was a good thing she had been able to get a shot off. His injuries weren't life-threatening, and he'd stand trial.

Clint kissed her temple, and she asked, "Any chance we can talk about happier things? Like, what do you think about a trip this winter to someplace warm, maybe Hawaii?"

He playfully tugged her chin. "I'm not sure your new best bud will want to let you out of his sight."

"Who? Jed? Are you kidding? I've almost got him talked into asking Maggie out on a date." Clint was right about one thing; she and Jed had gotten very close during the time they had been in the cave. Her ex didn't give them any credit for the ability to outsmart him.

He gave a low whistle. "Filler Up Diner, Maggie? He's been pining for her ever since he got to town."

She smacked her hand against her leg and grinned. "Exactly my point. He needs to make his move before some other man discovers how great she is and swoops in."

He kissed the top of her head. "So now you've moved from gardener to matchmaker?"

She enjoyed their banter and enthusiastically said, "Heck, yeah. Everyone needs to be as happy as we are."

Clint sat them both up straight and faced her. "Polly, if I could have stopped him before he kidnapped you, I would have. But I never would have guessed he was the true villain in all of this."

She thought about how she had misjudged her ex-husband right from the very beginning. How could she have made such a horrible error in judgment, one that might have cost her life if it hadn't been for these people at this ranch? People who had become family.

"My life was more like a film where the spouse is trying to convince the wife she was crazy even when she knew she wasn't."

A lump lodged in her throat and she was determined to push it back. She had built a dam against a waterfall of tears, and she didn't need it to break. Clint pulled her to his chest.

"You can cry for as long and as hard as you want. Being strong around me is a waste of energy. I want you to deal with what happened so that we can have our happy ending."

That was the undoing of the dam. Not only did a trickle start, but soon a rushing torrent like the spring thaw was unleashed. The sobs racked her body and Clint never let go. He continued to murmur she was safe. Together, they'd stand against whatever difficulties might come their way. And just as important, he would be by her side in court when she had to testify.

She sobbed until she felt the cracks of her heart coming together. Inside where the water and loneliness had eroded her heart, now her healing tears filled in the cracks and she became whole again. But she hadn't done it alone. Clint remained steadfast for as long as it had taken.

He withdrew a dark-blue bandana from inside his denim jacket and said, "Dry your eyes, darlin'. That's the last time you're going to waste tears because of the ex."

She took the well-worn cloth and wiped her face. To some it might have sounded like a command, but to her his voice was as steady as the mountains, support that was given from the depth of his heart. Clint was right. She was done crying for a man who never deserved her tears. The one who would never break her heart.

She settled back in his arms and drifted off to a dreamless sleep.

~

*A*nother week had passed, and Polly's house was finally put back together. It was time to ask Clint a very important question. With a glance at the kitchen clock, she pulled the potatoes from the oven and had the grill ready for the steak. One thing about ranching country, steak never tasted any better.

She heard the quick toot of his truck horn and she hurried out to the front porch where she stood on the top step and greeted him with a smile and open arms. "Hey, cowboy. 'Bout time you showed up. I was thinking I was going to be stood up."

He kissed her, causing her knees to buckle, and he laughed. "I stopped at the diner and picked up dessert." From inside the truck, he withdrew a white pastry box.

She tried to peek inside, and he closed the lid. With a wink, he said, "Later."

With her heart quickening, she tried to look away so

her eyes wouldn't betray she had something up her sleeve. "Come on in. But before dinner, I wanted to show you something."

Taking her hand, they climbed the steps and entered the cabin. The smell of fresh baked bread and roasted vegetables teased the taste buds. At least they did Polly's and Clint had a hearty appetite, so she knew it did the same for him.

"Would you put the box down on the coffee table and come with me? I need a minute of your help."

His brow arched, he watched as she opened the bedroom door.

"I've got a problem with the dresser and was hoping you could fix it."

His eyes twinkled. "I wasn't sure what you needed, but I'm happy to take a look."

At first glance, the room looked same, but he was noticing some differences. Some of her perfume bottles were missing from the dresser top and the stack of books that normally sat on the bedside table were missing too. "Darlin', did I miss some of the damage to your things when the house was ransacked?"

Her grin widened and her entire body swayed from side to side as she said, "Nope."

"Okay." The word came out as a drawl. "Then which drawer needs to be fixed?"

"Top left and the next one down." He couldn't get over why she looked happy that her dresser had been broken. But he opened the top drawer, and it slid open and closed smoothly. He did the same with the next one. Now he was confused. They were in fine condition.

"Polly, what am I missing? They're working just fine."

Now she giggled like a schoolgirl. "What's in them?"

He opened the top drawer again and felt around inside. "Nothing."

She crossed the room and pulled open the closet door, and it was only half-full. Her clothes were hanging neatly on the right and the left was empty. A thought came and went. It couldn't be.

"Clint, don't you find it a little odd that a woman would only use half her dresser and closet space?"

The little minx. Was she about to blow his carefully devised plan?

"If you want to leave half the space empty, that's your prerogative. It's your house, after all." Two could play at this game. And he was going to have a bit of fun now that he figured it out. "I'm going to put the steak on since I didn't need to be the handyman tonight. I'm not as accomplished as Quinn, but I'll do my best."

He strode out of the bedroom, doing his best to contain his laughter. After he had gotten three steps ahead of her, Polly came out of her bedroom and closed the door a little harder than she needed to.

"Clint Goodman, you're about as curious as a stick of firewood." She stomped around the kitchen, slamming cabinet doors and drawers as she pulled out plates and silverware.

It was all he could do to keep from laughing out loud. "I forgot the dessert in the living room. I'll be right back."

He noticed she glanced over her shoulder and her eyes narrowed. She was the curious one of the two. There was no way around it. With box in hand, he brought it into the kitchen. "I'll just slide the box into the refrigerator until we're ready."

She took the box but didn't open it. "Hold on there. Why does it need to be kept cold?"

"Maggie made some fancy desserts today. She's trying out new recipes, and I said we'd be happy to be her taste testers." He kept his crossed fingers behind his back. For a man who prided himself on being forthright, he was taking liberties with the truth now.

"On second thought, I've always thought dessert should be enjoyed before the main course." Her look was challenging. She popped the top and then closed it again. "What do you think? Care to join me?"

He grabbed two dinner plates and forks. "Sure, we can eat steak anytime."

Shock flitted over her face as he called her bluff. He pulled out her chair, and she sat down. He took the box from her hands and opened it. There were three different options, two of each: a tiny cream puff drizzled with chocolate, a chocolate and coconut frosted cupcake, and a small apple hand pie.

"What would you like to sample first?"

She grinned. "The cream puff."

"Excellent choice."

She dipped her fork in and cut it in half, making a perfect four bite confection. Pushing around the cream filling, she looked up through her eyelashes. "Is yours the same?"

Clint made quick work of the puff. "Yes, and it's a keeper for sure."

She leaned back in the chair and enjoyed the treat. When she was done, she carefully looked at the remaining two and that devilish grin came back. "The cupcake this time."

Once again, he placed the mini cupcake in the middle of her plate and smothered a smile as she cut it into two pieces of gooey cake and coconut.

"This is another keeper; don't you think, darlin'?"

She finished it off and said with a slight frown, "Let's have the pie, and then we'll cook dinner."

"Is dessert before dinner not as good as you thought?" He couldn't help but tease her since she had started this game with the dresser.

Inspecting the hand pie, she said, "Apple's never been my favorite, but I'll give it a try. Maggie is incredible in the kitchen."

"Apple is one of my favorites." This time he let her take one and, just as he suspected, she selected the pie that was closest to him.

She cut it up like the others. "I don't think the apples are completely cooked."

"Let me see." He reached over and picked up her plate. Moving the fork slightly, it went through like a hot knife and butter. "Here you go." He handed her back the plate.

She scooped up a forkful and stopped before it reached her face. "It's really just a personal-sized pie."

He scraped the last of the pie filling from the plate and grinned. "Dessert was excellent. Maggie will definitely have to add these to her menu, even if they are for special occasions."

Polly smiled and got up. "I'm going to get the steak out and maybe you can start the grill?"

He placed the plates in the sink, keeping one eye on Polly and the other on the brown paper. He had gone to special trouble to tie it up with butcher's twine and, after struggling for less than a minute, she snipped it with scissors.

"Good thing we had a snack. We won't be eating dinner until tomorrow at this rate."

"I've got time." He kissed her neck and felt her melt into him.

Folding back the paper, she heard a soft clang of something hitting the granite counter. Her mouth formed a large O as she picked up the ring off the counter.

Before she could say a word, Clint plucked the antique diamond ring out of her fingers and held it up. Her face was as bright as the northern lights.

"Polly, from the moment I found you on that hiking trail, I didn't know a thing about you, but you drew me to you. It was as if after all these years I had found my place, my home. I've loved you from the day you stepped foot on the ranch and I will love you until I take my last breath. And if you'll allow me the honor of moving my clothes into those empty drawers and closet in there, I will spend the rest of my life being the kind of man you are proud to call your husband."

Sliding the ring on her finger, he waited for what she had to say.

Tears gathered in her eyes. "I discovered I didn't need to hide anymore but I've found my home in Montana with you. During those days in the hospital, your voice gave me hope I would find my future. I came to River Junction to build a life and I've found love. I can't wait to start our life together."

He took her in his arms and lowered his lips to hers. "Darlin', we already have."

If you loved **Hiding in Montana** help other readers find this book: **Please leave a review now!**
Are you ready to read more about the Price family? Check

out this sneak peek at Breathe, Book 1 in the Price Family set at Crescent Lake Winery series:

Her dream come true may be the end of his…

Her family's successful winery business in a small town in upstate New York should have gone to Tessa Price. She'd always dreamed of running the winery, but her brother, the prodigal son, has returned to claim the corner office. Looking to prove to her family she's more than capable, she boldly strikes out on her own, purchasing Sand Creek Winery—a cash-strapped competitor—right out from under her family. She can forge her own destiny, using her marketing skills and big plans to bring new life to the small winery. But first she has a proposition for the sexy previous owner. And he's likely to hate it almost as much as he hates anyone with the last name of Price.

Kevin "Max" Maxwell would never have willingly sold his winery to anyone named Price. Family always comes first, and if paying for his sister's cancer treatment cost him his business, it was worth it. But when the new owner offers him a one-year contract to stay on as general manager, with a possible bonus, he's hit rock bottom but he really can't afford to turn it down. He can ignore the effect her deep brown eyes and heart-shaped face have on his senses for a year, can't he?

Relationships, like slowly ripening vineyards, take time. But Max has been keeping a secret from Tessa, one that could destroy their hopes for a future. Will a terrible accident force Tessa and Max to face how much they have to lose or tear apart their budding relationship forever?

Sometimes a romance is like a fine wine. To be its best, it just needs time to breathe.

Keep reading for a sneak peek of
Breathe-
Price Family Romance Series
Featuring the amazing Tessa Price and the dashing
Kevin, Max, Maxwell
Order Now

LUCINDA RACE

BREATHE

Price Family Romance Series

CHAPTER ONE

The moment Tessa opened the heavy wood and glass door, her eyes were drawn to the tall, open stairwell. Kevin Maxwell leaned against the steel and glass banister, watching her.

He greeted her with a flat smile. "Good morning, Ms. Price. Welcome to Sand Creek Winery."

The glass door closed behind her with a small whoosh. She squared her shoulders and walked into her winery. "Please call me Tessa."

He gave her a half nod. "Tessa."

"I'm glad you're here. I wanted to talk with you."

"I've been clearing out my"—he gave a slow shake of his head—"your office. I won't be long."

She ascended the stairwell. "Wait."

Kevin's cool blue eyes met hers. He was dressed casually in a crisp, cream-colored shirt, the cuffs rolled back, which highlighted strong hands and muscled forearms. He had high cheekbones, a long, thin nose, and was more handsome up close. She guessed he was around her age.

"I'd like to start our relationship on the right foot."

His eyes never left hers. Challenging her.

She had been right that he wasn't thrilled to see her. She had negotiated the purchase through a broker since she suspected he wouldn't sell to a Price, no matter how much money was involved. She'd made a fair offer and he'd accepted it.

She pointed to an open door. "After you."

He did a one-eighty and strode through the doorway.

The large room was dominated by a long maple conference table and several leather chairs. In front of her was a wall of windows that looked out over acre after acre of vines. Pride surged in her. It already felt like she belonged. Several boxes were strewn about, in various stages of being packed. Not seeing a desk, she set her black leather briefcase on the table and walked to the windows.

"Quite the view." Kevin had come to stand next to her. He was so close, she could feel the waves of indifference radiating off him.

Without looking at him, she said, "It looks completely different from this perspective. The virtual tour didn't do it justice."

"When I built this building, my intent was to be able to look out and witness nature as it nurtures the vines. Watching the vineyard throughout the seasons gives me hope for the future. There's nothing like it." He turned away as if he couldn't bear to look any longer.

"Impressive." She was reminded of the view in Don's office. It was strikingly similar. She turned from the window and gestured to the chairs at the table. "Please, can we talk?"

He dropped to a wooden stool, leaving the executive chair noticeably empty.

Unsure where to start, she said, "You can trust me with

Sand Creek Winery." She empathized with how it must feel, forced to sell his business.

When she sat down, he gave her a curious look. "It was either accept the blind offer or let the bank take it. I'll admit if I had known it was a Price, I might have reconsidered."

She cocked her head to the side and let that comment slide. "I have a proposition for you." She wanted to rephrase that, but it was already out there.

His eyebrow rose and his chin dropped a fraction of an inch. "I'm listening."

"I would like for you to stay on as the general manager."

She could have heard a pin drop.

"And why would I want to do that?"

She leaned forward and clasped her hands, resting them on the polished wooden surface. "You're a good winemaker. I suspect a good marketing campaign can change sales. I happen to excel in sales and marketing."

"You think very highly of yourself."

She thought she saw a glimmer of humor in his crystal-blue eyes. "You know how to manage the field workers. You have a couple of excellent wines, but I want to hire an enologist to work with you, someone who is interested in growing this business."

Kevin leaned back in the chair and crossed his arms over his chest. "What's in it for me besides a paycheck?"

Available on all storefronts, *be sure to pick up your copy today*. Order Breathe- Book 1
Price Family Romance Series
Order Now

A FREE STORY FOR YOU

Have you enjoyed Hiding in Montana? Not ready to stop reading yet? If you sign up for my newsletter at www. lucindarace.com/newsletter you will receive Blends, the love story of Sam and Sherry, right away as my thank-you gift for choosing to get my newsletter.

Can two hearts blend together for a life long love..

His mother's final illness waylaid Sam Price's college dreams, but he's content working in his family's vineyard in a small town in upstate New York. When he finds a woman with a flat tire on a vineyard road, he's stunned to discover it's the girl he'd had a crush on in high school. He'd never been confident enough to ask her out back then. He'd been a farm kid. Her daddy was the bank president. Way out of his league.

Sherry Jones is tired of her parents' ambitious plans for her life. She'll finish her college accounting degree like they want, but how can she tell them about her real love:

working with growing things? Then a flat tire and a neglected garden offer her an unexpected opportunity, with the added bonus of a tall, gorgeous guy with eyes that set her senses tingling.

What does a guy with dirt under his nails and calluses on his hands have to offer a woman like Sherry? It will take courage for her to defy her parents and claim her own dreams. Sam and Sherry's lives took different paths, but a winding vineyard road has brought them back together. Are they willing to take a chance to create the perfect blend for a lifelong love?

Blends is only available by signing up for my newsletter – sign up for it here at www.lucindarace.com/newsletter

LUCINDA RACE

BLENDS

a crescent lake winery novella

SNEAK PEEK

Chapter One

Early 1980's... Sherry Jones kicked the gravel road with the toe of her bright-pink sandal. Pebbles flew across the road to the scrubby grass on the other side. A flat tire and she was in the middle of nothing but grapevines. She turned three hundred and sixty degrees. As far as the eye could see, vines.

Why did it have to be so damn hot today? It was spring, not mid-July or August. A trickle of sweat ran down her back. Whether she went right or left, it was going to be a long, hot walk. She knew how far the gas station was from the direction she had come from, so it was time to go the opposite way. She couldn't remember ever being in this part of Crescent Lake before. Surely she'd find a house or a gas station that was closer down this road, and hopefully someone would be around so she could use the phone.

She jammed her keys in her distressed short-shorts pocket and walked at a steady pace. She hadn't gone more than a quarter of a mile when a blister began to form between her big toe and the thong. In the distance, she could hear the faint rumble of thunder, or was that a truck? If it was a storm, could her spring break get any worse? Last week, she broke up with Brad the cheater, her boyfriend of all of three months, and now she had to deal with a flat on her new used car, and a blister. She kicked off her sandals and walked in the sparse grass on the side of the road. There was a break in the never-ending field: another dirt road. The rumbling grew closer. A pickup truck slowed and came to a halt.

Her day just got worse. Arrogant and obnoxious, Sam Price stopped and leaned out the driver's window. "Well, look at you."

He flashed her a wide smile, his teeth even brighter against his tanned skin. She guessed it was from working outside all day. She hated to ask, but getting help was better than walking for miles, and it wasn't like he was the worst guy in the world. Just, they weren't friends.

"Hi, Sam." She shaded her eyes with her hand. "Any chance you know how to change a tire?"

"Sherry Jones, of all people to find wandering in my vineyard; of course I do. You don't drive around in trucks all day without knowing how to do simple repairs." His smile was broad, and his tone was slightly cocky.

She put a hand on her hip and glared at him. "Well, not everyone drives around in trucks all day." She wanted to snap at him but if she did, there'd be no way he'd help change her tire.

"Touché." He shrugged. "I'm gonna take off. See ya around." He looked toward the road in front of him. With a wave of his hand, he dropped the truck into gear and eased forward.

She groaned. "Sam. Wait."

He turned to her. His lips twitched as the smile grew wide.

"I'm sorry. Is there any chance you have time to change my tire?" She jerked her thumb over her shoulder. "My car is back that way and the passenger side is flat as a pancake."

He propped his arm in the open window and pointed to the seat. "Hop in."

She tossed the offending thong in the truck and climbed inside. "Thanks. I appreciate you taking the time to help."

He gave her a sidelong look. "Why are you limping?"

"Blister. My sandals aren't made for walking any distance."

"Just for looks?"

Was that his way of paying her a compliment or was he being a smart aleck? "Something like that."

He threw the truck in reverse with a slight jerk and did a three-point turn to go back in the direction she had come from. She wasn't sure what to say to make small talk. They bumped over the dirt road without talking. He whistled off-key, and she stared out the windshield.

"Thanks again for helping. I'm sure you're busy."

"I've got time." He pointed to a car off to the side of the road. "Is that you?"

She nodded.

"Glad to see you pulled off the road."

Annoyance bubbled up. "Do you think I'd just leave it so no one could get around?"

He held up a hand. "It's a dirt road. Not many people come this way." He looked at her. "What are you doing out here?"

"Just driving around." The last thing she was going to

tell him was the real reason she was driving through endless miles of grapevines. She was hiding from the world.

He pulled off and parked. "Pop the trunk so we can get the jack and spare."

He walked next to her. She couldn't help but notice he had grown taller since graduation but he still had those molten brown eyes, long eyelashes, and bleached-blond hair. Even though he had a hat and sunglasses on, she remembered them and him. He was easy on the eyes, and all the girls had thought so in high school.

She unlocked the trunk and the lid sprang open. He lifted up the tire well. It was empty. She felt the color drain from her face. Now what? No spare and she was stuck.

"Sherry, what are you doing driving around without a spare tire?"

She threw up her hands. "How should I know? I just bought this car when I got home for spring break. Don't they always have them?"

He flicked the trunk closed and leaned against it. He pushed his ballcap back and propped his sunglasses on the brim. His deep-brown eyes were fixed on her.

"Did you check the trunk when you took it for a test drive?"

Crossing her arms over her chest, she said, "No." She tilted her chin up.

"You can't assume when you're buying a used car." He kicked some stones with his work boot, causing little puffs of dust to float in the air. He looked down the road as if weighing his options. "Get your stuff and I'll drive you home. But I need to stop at my house first. You can use the phone to call a tow truck."

"I don't want to put you out. I'll call my mom and she can pick me up."

He seemed to consider what he wanted to say next and gave her a sidelong look. "I'll drive you into town. I need to go to the hardware store anyway." He walked around to the driver's door and opened it. "But the tow truck can be on its way out here and you could get your car back tomorrow. Leave the keys under the mat and we can get going."

She didn't move. "Are you sure the car is safe with the keys in it?" She pursed her lips. She had been saving for the last three years to buy her first car and she didn't want to have it stolen. Her hard work would have been for nothing if that happened. Besides, in two short months, she would need it to drive to her first full-time job.

"Out here, we'd leave our keys in the ignition with a flat. No one would bother it. Your car is safe."

She looked from Sam to her car. It wasn't that she didn't want to believe him but— "I'm not sure."

He extended his hand but it never contacted hers. In spite of that lack of touch, the racing sensation down her arm felt like he had. His voice softened. "Trust me. If someone steals your wheels, I'll replace it."

"Well, that wouldn't be necessary." She looked at him. It felt like it was the first time she was seeing Sam. It was a cliché, but if eyes were the window to the soul, this brash guy had a gentle side. "Alright." She took her bookbag and rolled up the windows and then placed the keys underneath and in the center of the rubber floor mat.

***

Sam waited for her before he walked back to his truck. "I have to swing by the house before we head into town. I need to get my list for the hardware store. Now, when we

249

get to my place, don't worry about the dogs. They're big and bark a lot but they're harmless."

When he had seen Sherry walking barefoot down the dirt road, her shoulders slumped, he had to stop and help. She was the one girl he had wanted to date in high school but had never asked. She was out of his league. Her mom was a high school English teacher and her dad was the president of a bank in Syracuse. His family worked the land. Not that he was ashamed that his fingernails had dirt under them and there were calluses on the palms of his hands. They had a great life and he wouldn't trade it for anything, but she was out of his dating pool.

"When we get to the house, I'll get you something to put on your blister. You don't want to have it pop and get infected."

"Sam, you don't need to fuss over me." Her long blond ponytail swung from side to side. She looked like she was barely sixteen.

"How's college?"

"Two more months and then I have to start working full time."

He nodded as they drove. "Any ideas?"

"Office job. I'll have a degree in accounting, but it is so boring." She rolled her eyes.

With a chuckle, he asked, "Then why are you studying it?" He gave her a side-glance.

"My parents think it's a sound career choice. I might take the CPA exam."

"What's that?" He couldn't imagine not doing what he wanted to every day. It was like he had grape juice in his veins instead of blood. He loved the winemaking business. The ups and downs of a growing season, it was the ultimate thrill ride. This was something he wanted to do until he took his last breath.

"Certified public accountant." She released a heavy sigh. "I can become a controller for a company or something like that."

"I take it that's not for you." He saw the look of resignation on her face.

"I'll make a decent living, but doesn't it sound dull to go to an office every day for the next forty-plus years?"

Now he was curious. "What would you do if you could?"

She looked out the side window and waved her hand, trying to dismiss the question. "You'll laugh."

"Come on. Try me." Now he had to know. "If you tell me, I'll share a secret with you."

She gave him a curious look. He could tell she was trying to decide if she should or not.

"Landscape horticulturist."

It came out almost as a whisper.

She liked plants. He grinned. They had something in common after all. "Then why aren't you studying horticulture? Growing anything is gratifying." He pointed out the window to the passing landscape. "Look around you." The vines gave way to the long driveway leading to his parents' house. His mom always had beautiful flower gardens, but since she had passed away, they had become neglected.

Stately maple trees lined part of the drive as they grew closer to the house. "Don't look too close at the flower beds; they've been neglected the last couple of years."

Sherry's eyes were glued to them. Her eyes were bright as she saw the terraced gardens to the left of the road.

"Mom has, had, her vegetables there. She always had a

huge garden and preserved a lot of what she grew. She also gave bushels of vegetables to the field workers each season." He smiled, remembering the baskets he'd have to lug down to the warehouses each afternoon after she harvested. Well, that was before he got involved with working in the fields to learn about the cultivation of grapes from Dad.

"Your mom doesn't garden anymore?"

"I guess you didn't hear." His hand tightened on the steering wheel and he swallowed the lump in his throat. "She died. Cancer." It still burned and probably always would.

She touched his arm with a featherlike gesture. "I'm sorry. I didn't know."

"It's just me and Dad now." He stopped the truck and looked at her. She curled her fingers into the palm of her hand. Silence filled the cab for the few moments they sat there. He could still feel the warmth of her touch.

He cleared his throat and mumbled, "Thanks." He pushed open the door. "Come on in."

She followed him to the back door. Two large German shepherds came racing around the corner at full speed. The scream died in her throat. They jumped against her and pushed her back. She stumbled. Sam put his arm out to catch her, but she still landed on her butt. They continued to bark. She cringed.

"Doc. Moe. Sit." Sam snapped his fingers. The barking ceased.

She was surprised to see the dogs' butts on the ground, and then they lay down, their heads resting on their paws. Sam extended his hand and pulled her to her feet.

"They won't hurt you."

In a few flicks, she brushed off her backside and straightened her top.

She glanced at them, suspicious. "Their teeth don't look harmless."

"They love people." He knelt on the ground and spoke quietly. Their ears twitched. "This is Sherry and she's my friend. Be nice."

She wasn't sure which dog was which, but first one's tail began to thump on the ground and then the other.

He looked up at her. "Do you want to pet them?"

She wasn't a dog person. Her parents had an old cat who spent her days and nights snoozing. Sherry was cautious but knelt on the ground in front of the dogs, feeling confident because of the way Sam looked at her. He had an intensity about him. Her pulse quickened and her eyes locked on his. "Okay," she breathed. But what she had just agreed to was anyone's guess.

Blends is only available by signing up for my newsletter – sign up for it here at www.lucindarace.com/newsletter

LOVE TO READ?

CHECK OUT MY OTHER BOOKS

Cowboys of River Junction

Stars Over Montana

The cowboy broke her heart but he never stopped loving her. Now she's back ready to run her grandfather's ranch...

Hiding in Montana

Orchard Brides Series

Apple Blossoms in Montana

Twenty years later Renee and Hank are back where they fell in love but reality is like a spring frost and is a long-distance relationship their only option for their second chance?

The Sandy Bay Series

Sundaes on Sunday

A widowed school teacher and the airline pilot whose little girl is determined to bring her daddy and the lady from the ice cream shop together for a second chance at love.

Last Man Standing/Always a Bridesmaid
Barrett
Has the last man standing finally met his match?

Marie *May 2023*
Career focused city girl discovers small town charm can lead to love.

The Crescent Lake Winery Series
Breathe
Her dream come true may be the end of his...

Crush
The first time they met was fleeting, the second time restarted her heart.

Blush
He's always loved her but he left and now he's back...the question, does she still love him?

Vintage
He's an unexpected distraction, she gets his engine running...

Bouquet
Sweet second chances for a widow and the handsome billionaire...

Holiday Romance
The Sugar Plum Inn
The chef and the restaurant critic are about to come face to face.

Last Chance Beach
Shamrocks are a Girl's Best Friend
Will a bit of Irish luck and a matchmaking uncle give Kelly and Tric a chance to find love?

A Dickens Holiday Romance
Holiday Heart Wishes
Heartfelt wishes and holiday kisses...

Holly Berries and Hockey Pucks
Hockey, holidays, and a slap shot to the heart.

Christmas in July
She's the hometown girl with the hometown advantage. Right?

A Secret Santa Christmas
Christmas just isn't Holly's thing, but will a family secret help her find the true meaning of Christmas?

It's Just Coffee Series 2020
The Matchmaker and The Marine
She vowed never to love again. His career in the Marines crushed his ability to love. Can undeniable chemistry and a leap of faith overcome their past?

The MacLellan Sisters Trilogy
Old and New
An enchanted heirloom wedding dress and a letter change three sisters lives forever as they fulfill their grandmothers last request try on the dress.

Borrowed
He's just a borrowed boyfriend. He might also be her true love.

Blue
Will an enchanted wedding dress work its magic one more time?

The Loudon Series
Between Here and Heaven
Ten years of heaven on earth dissolved in an instant for Cari McKenna when her husband Ben died.

Lost and Found
Love never ends... A widow who talks to her late husband and

her handsome single neighbor who has secretly loved her for years.

The Journey Home

Where do you go to heal your heart? You make the journey home...

The Last First Kiss

When life handed Kate lemons, she baked.

Ready to Soar

Kate will fight for love, won't she?

Love in the Looking Glass

Will Ellie's first love be her last or will she become a ghost like her father?

Magic in the Rain

Dani's plan of hiding in plain sight may not have been the best idea.

Cozy Mystery Books

A Bookstore Cozy Mystery Series 2023

Books & Bribes

It was an ordinary day until the book of Practical Magic conked Lily on the head causing her to see stars. And then she discovered her cat, Milo, could talk.

Catnip & Crimes

Tea & Trouble

Scares & Dares

SOCIAL MEDIA

Follow Me on Social Media

Like my Facebook page
Join Lucinda's Heart Racer's Reader Group on Facebook
Twitter @lucindarace
Instagram @lucindraceauthor
BookBub
Goodreads
Pinterest

ABOUT THE AUTHOR

Award-winning and best-selling author Lucinda Race is a lifelong fan of reading. As a young girl, she spent hours reading novels and getting lost in the fun and hope they represent. While her friends dreamed of becoming doctors and engineers, her dreams were to become a writer—a novelist.

As life twisted and turned, she found herself writing nonfiction but longed to turn to her true passion. After developing the storyline for A McKenna Family Romance, it was time to start living her dream. Her fingers practically fly over computer keys as she weaves stories of mystery and romance.

Lucinda lives with her two little dogs, a miniature long hair dachshund and a shih tzu mix rescue, in the rolling hills of western Massachusetts. When she's not at her day job, she's immersed in her fictional worlds. And if she's not writing romance or cozy mystery novels, she's reading everything she can get her hands on.

9 781954 520424